LIQUID REGRET

BOOK 1 IN THE LIQUID REGRET SERIES

BY MJ CARNAL

The book is intended for mature audiences only.

Cover Model: Joshua Sean McCann

Cover Photographer: FuriousFotog

Cover Designer: Cover Me, Darling

Editor: Kellie Montgomery

Dedication

To Nathan, my "official song writer" for Liquid Regret. Your words inspire me.

To my readers. THANK YOU will never be enough for taking this journey with me.

Chapter 1

I want so much to heal your pain, the wounds, the hurt, it's all in vain. Regret is deep and stings like rain, like an open wound Without Novocain." - Liquid Regret

One year. Three hundred and sixty five agonizing days. It feels like a lifetime. Her emerald eyes haunt me. I dream about her on the nights I actually get to sleep. I've turned into a total pussy. Twelve months ago, I watched her walk away from me and did nothing to stop her. She was never mine to begin with but that hasn't stopped me from obsessing over the next time I'll see her. What the hell is wrong with me? Yep, total pussy.

We've spent the last six months on a tour bus, hopping from city to city, hotel to hotel. I've searched for replacements but no one has come even remotely close. Being the lead singer of the hottest band in the US right now, I have my choice of women every night. I step off stage and there they are. It's like a buffet that's laid out just for me. All shapes, all sizes, I can take my pick. Each one of them offers me exactly what I want, exactly how I want it. The problem? No one can give me what I need. No one but her.

"D Rey, come back to bed."

Tonight's replacement looks more like Mia. Her red hair is long and straight but her skin isn't as soft. Her eyes aren't as green. She stretches and smiles at me. I've got to get her out of here. She's stayed longer than I usually allow them to and she's got to go. The walls are starting to close in on me. What the fuck was her name? Michelle? No, that's not right. Melissa? No. I'm an asshole.

Don't judge me. I'm a man. Being on stage is a huge high and there's nothing better than losing myself inside a woman to bring me down from that. I don't have the luxury of having a drink or popping a pill. Those days are long gone. I've been clean for fourteen years. Aside from the occasional aspirin, my body is chemical free and Mia Avery Lee is my only drug. Fucking her out of my system is the cure. It hasn't worked yet. But, eventually it has to.

A year ago, I helped my cousin propose to the love of his life. Ironically, she'd been my girlfriend first. She dumped me the second good ole Steve gave her the time of day. That's a story I will gag through later. You should probably get to know me first.

They say your past defines you. I call bullshit on that. I've spent the last ten years ensuring that mine doesn't. I've lost my way lately but the last decade has seen living on the street, rolling in money and everything in between.

"D Rey, baby. Let me make you feel good again." Time's up. Her voice is like nails on a chalkboard. I don't understand the whining. I don't handle that well.

"You need to go before my manager storms through this door and rips my dick off." I'm pleading now but she isn't moving. "We're leaving for the West Coast in the morning and I need to get my shit together."

This woman is another mistake in a huge line of mistakes in my life. Let's get all the judgment over at once, shall we? Where should I start? I had a fucked up childhood. My dad sucked and spent more time pummeling me than he did sleeping. I fell into the wrong crowd in high school and spent my time shooting up or looking for anything that would make me numb. My aunt and uncle saved me, got me clean, got the dealer off my back and loved me when I needed it most. Looking back, getting clean may have been the easy part. I was 16 and my hormones were everywhere. I thought with my dick. What kid in high school doesn't? When a cheerleader gave me the time of day at a party, I jumped at it. A couple months later, she was at my doorstep with a pregnancy test that changed everything.

I panicked. Can you blame me? Her parents were self-important and couldn't stand to be embarrassed. She told them I had raped her. Who are you going to believe? Claire, the honor roll cheerleader or Damien, the recovering drug addict? I begged her to tell the truth and when she saw the beating my dad had given me that night, she admitted she'd lied. It was too late. The damage had been done. Dear ole dad said he was going to take things out on my mom. Hearing her crying that whole night was too much for me. He hadn't laid a hand on her but the verbal abuse was enough to make me want to kill him. I thought the only way to save her was to disappear. So, that night, while the rest of the world was asleep, I packed the few things I owned and took off.

I kept in touch with Claire and was able to sneak into the hospital and get a glimpse of my son the night he was born. If you think parenthood doesn't have a profound impact on a teenager, think again. Suddenly, everything made sense. Xander Bennet changed everything. I learned some important lessons that night. The dick that had been labeled as my father wasn't even worth pissing on had he been on fire. How anyone could hurt a child was something I would never understand. Claire became my family forever, whether I wanted that or not. And I learned how much I needed and missed my cousin and my insane group of friends.

Still, going home wasn't an option. My dad had gotten sick and he blamed the cancer on me and my mom. No way was I adding to that hell storm. I kept moving, finding shelter, food, whatever else I needed. I refused to give up. I met Griffin while I was living on the street. He was only a year older but his story was similar to mine. He let me sleep on his ripped up sofa in the shit smelling apartment he was able to afford. He and his girlfriend, Della, became my family. We bonded over music and Griff and I started to form what later became Liquid Regret. He's known to the world as Harley. It's a long story that involves the paparazzi and his motorcycle but that's his story to tell. Della is now his wife. He's a lucky son of a bitch. They inspire me to find that for myself. They've been married for two years but have loved each other since the beginning of time.

I won't deny that I'm the playboy of the group. I suck and I know it. But I need sex like I need to breathe. Sure, I traded one addiction for another but the only way I can get through this crazy life out here on the road is to find one thing that's the same in every city. Without a doubt, that's the women. So what if I find myself on the front of every gossip rag? I've been called a womanizer, a cheater, a playboy, you name it, they've said it. It's not 100% true but it's pretty fucking close. I'd trade it all for Mia but I don't see that happening. The person my lifestyle hurts the most is Xander. I don't get to see him anymore. Claire said I'd have to give up touring and women and settle down. It makes me a douche that I won't do it but it's the only way I can support my son and give him the financial security he deserves. Once I'm back in LA, shit will change. For now, he's better off with his mom.

See? I'm a fucked up mess. I have no one to blame but myself. Life happened so quickly, I didn't know whether to hold on tight or jump off before my sanity was completely shot. I fought so hard for fame that when I got it, I didn't know what to do with it. Our first big gig was the LA Music Awards and a tour as opening act for Ripping Pages. That lasted all of ten shows before our managers realized that the venues were selling out and we were their meal ticket. I'm not complaining. Liquid Regret is the hottest group in the US and being out on tour is everything I dreamed it would be. But somewhere in my dreams, I had imagined sleep and fast cars and so much money I could wipe my ass with it. I have the money, I just don't have a minute to myself to spend it. What I don't send to my son and the devil that won't let me see him, I'm stashing in hopes of settling down in LA near my family.

The Lee sisters were my ultimate undoing. I dated Lily for what amounted to less than a minute in the grand scheme of things. She was gorgeous and did things to my heart that no one else had. But, it wasn't ever quite right. There was always something missing. Little did I know that missing piece was her sister, Mia. She's fucking beautiful. Her skin smells good, her red hair reminds me of flames and I want to spend every second of my life worshiping her body.

The second I saw her, I took the first deep breath I'd taken in years.

They say that "the one" is supposed to take your breath away. That's crap. Mia walked in, took one look at me and smiled. I was done. I felt calm, I felt centered, I felt whole. Being in her presence made me realize that I hadn't been fully relaxed since I was a kid. The weight of the world shifted off my shoulders. She was it for me and I was too much of a pussy to realize how much that meant.

Lily noticed right away. She'd taken me home to meet her family. Not because we were a serious item but because she didn't want to travel cross country alone. I didn't have anything else going on so I jumped at the chance to spend that time with her. I was a fill in for my cousin, Steve. I was ok with that. She was hot and I was horny. When she saw the way I looked at Mia, she busted my balls relentlessly about being too scared to make a move. She was right. I was on the brink of my first tour. I didn't need anything serious if I was leaving. But I kissed her that trip and I felt it all the way to my toes.

My second trip home with Lil was different. We tried the dating thing, both of us looking for someone to fill the void. She was smarter than I was and let me down easy. I rushed into her Georgia apartment hoping Mia would be there. She was. Her loser ex-boyfriend greeted me too. That didn't stop me from tangling her hair around my fingers while I kissed her like a man on a mission. I spent the rest of that trip staring at her and following her around like a crazy stalker ready to kidnap my next victim. We had a couple great nights together. She was definitely too good for me and we kept things PG. But it was hard to walk out the last morning.

I promised I would leave two tickets for her at every show on the East Coast. She hadn't used any of them. I'd like to be a macho man and tell you that I didn't give a shit. I'd be lying.

"Shit." The pounding at my door is one of two people. Either my dick of a father got through security or my manager is pissed. Marie. That's it. I knew I'd figure it out. "Marie, get dressed."

Looking through the peep hole confirms what I already knew. It's Joshua Seymour, kick ass manager and resident pain in my balls. It's not entirely my fault that he's pissed. In all fairness, I didn't want to do the meet and great backstage. It's also not my fault that Marie was more into me than her burly boyfriend. It was a case of bad timing. She jumped into my arms and stuck her tongue down my throat before I even knew what the hell was happening. I was simply trying to defend her honor when I laid his ass out for charging at me. Sure, those vultures with the zoom lenses got some shots of me being the hero. Sue me. OK, don't. That's probably what ole Josh is worried about. I wasn't going to let him kick my ass in front of my fans.

"Welcome. What brings you by this late at night?" Think my innocent act will work? Probably not, judging by the look on Mr. Seymour's face. It certainly won't work with the security detail he brought along.

"You." He points his finger right at Marie, who hasn't made one attempt to remove herself from my bed. "Get your shit. Time to say goodbye."

"But.." Marie stutters as she searches the room for her other shoe.

"Gentlemen, please show Mr. Reynolds' guest out." Joshua pushes past me and points at me. "This is bad, Damien. Your reputation can't take much more of this. Her boyfriend wants to press charges. The paparazzi got shots of you two doing more than just innocent kissing or whatever that last bullshit story was about."

"So spin it. Like you've done all the rest." I swear I'm not trying to piss him off.

Joshua huffs before he sits down and presses his fingers to his temples. "Damien, we need to change your image. I don't know how, but the label says that I've got two options. Calm your ass down or find another face for Liquid Regret. We both know they're nothing without you."

Well this is a kick in the nuts. "I'm their cash cow, J."

"Maybe so. But I'm exhausted. Can we play by their rules for five minutes? Every single member of this band would leave the label before they let you go. We're talking breach of contract and uprooting family and God knows what else. I'm begging here, Damien. I'll spin this story but you may not like it. I need you to get your shit together."

I can't help but be scared shitless about how he might spin this but I've got to trust him. He's never done me wrong. "Spin away."

Chapter 2

"The man is hot as sin." Laney throws the paper down in front of me before stealing one of my fries. "And someone finally snatched him up. Hard to believe the playboy of the music world is finally settling down."

I feel like I'm going to throw up. The headline taunts me. I can't help myself. I have to pick up the paper and read it. "Liquid Regret's Lead Singer Meets His Match." The headline alone makes my head spin. "Damien 'D-Rey' Reynolds and Russian supermodel, Oksana Zolotov, to wed next fall."

"Holy shit." I whisper and stare at their picture.

"I know, right?" Laney takes a gulp of her diet soda and shakes her head. "It says they met a few months ago and have been serious ever since. It also says that the pictures of him with all those other women are either old or the media's attempt to break them up. Crazy. Lucky bitch."

In all fairness, I haven't told anyone about my feelings for Damien Moving to Los Angeles to be closer to my sister, Lily, was a fresh start for me. All my friends here just know me as easy going, laid back Mia Avery Lee. They aren't wrong. That's really who I am. But my brief affair with Damien Reynolds is something I keep hidden. It's a special memory and I'm not willing to share it.

I spent a week with him. One week that changed my life. My sister brought him home with her for her short lived move back to Georgia a year ago. They tried the dating thing but decided they were better off as friends. My connection with him was instant. My heart actually skipped the first time I saw him. I am a huge romantic and believe in love at first sight. I believe in happily ever after. I know that my prince will ride up on a white horse and take me away. I saw the complete picture the first time I looked into his eyes.

His eyes. Deep pools of aqua that I could lose myself in for the rest of my life. When he looked at me, I swear he saw right into my soul. His lips were soft and owned every part of me when we kissed. His strong arms wrapped around me and I was home. I knew it was short lived. He was the lead singer of the next big thing. His band was going out on tour and I knew he would have the world at his fingertips. I also knew that he would have women falling at his feet. If the gossip pages were true, my assumptions had been correct.

When he left me on that Sunday morning, he'd promised to leave tickets and back stage passes for me at every show near Georgia. I wanted to use them. I really did. The first time they were in town, I was still too consumed with all things Damien to use them. I spent weeks nursing a broken heart and it was just too soon. It wasn't long after that I got a job offer at the Aquarium of the Pacific and jumped at the chance. Working with the dolphins at the Atlanta Aquarium had been a dream. I was able to put my degree in marine biology to work and I'd been happy. When I got the call from Los Angeles, I couldn't turn it down. I was going to be able to work with sea otters and seals and travel to rescue different animals. With a deep breath and no way to contact Damien, I began the cross country journey to my new life.

It was stupid to not exchange phone numbers. I just thought it would be easier. I was turning things over to fate and if they were meant to be, they would be. Romance at its finest. Like I said, I'm a romantic. I vowed not to ask my sister or her fiancé for his number. Lily was marrying Damien's cousin, Steve. I'd heard things over the past year. I knew the tour was going well and I knew that Damien and Steve talked once a week. But I never asked any questions. Steve would tell different stories about the tour when we all got together for dinner but no one knew what I was feeling. I'm a pretty private person and I don't like the world to see me heartbroken. That doesn't mean that I haven't kept up with Liquid Regret's touring schedule and watched entertainment shows and red carpet interviews. I guess I just like to torture myself in private.

"Earth to Mia. You're crying. What's wrong?"

I hadn't realized I was crying until Laney took my hand. She'd quickly become my best friend in California. She worked in conservation education at the aquarium and helped teach children the importance of keeping the environment clean.

"It's stupid." I feel like a complete fool. I'm typically not a crier but here I sit, at work, losing my cool. "I'm just a romantic. I love a good love story."

"So it has nothing to do with the mystery woman that got away?" Laney winks at me before she laughs. "Rumor is that there's a red head that he spent the summer with and he calls her the one that got away. The other part of the rumor is that she lived in Atlanta and he was with her until the day they went on tour."

"Shit." Covering my eyes, I try to hide from the world. Maybe the floor will open up and suck me in so I don't have to answer any questions. How in the hell is there a rumor and I haven't heard it?

"You slut!" She laughs so hard that I can't help but blush. "It's you. I knew it. You're always on the lookout for anything having to do with Liquid Regret and I see it in your eyes every time you look at his picture. Holy shit. I can't believe this."

"Lane, swear to me that this stays between us. No one else can know. It was a quick summer fling and I don't want all the questions or the attention."

"Pinkie promise. But you're telling me the whole story. Drinks on Friday?" Laney grabs her bag and throws it over her shoulder. "You're my hero, Miml."

Once she walks away, I realize how alone I really am. When I first moved to LA, I stayed with Lily and Steve. It was so much fun and we stayed up way too late every night. Once I started working, it made more sense to rent an apartment close to the aquarium. The rent is perfect and the one bedroom provides just enough room for me and my memories. I need to get out more. I need to meet more people. I need to start dating. Now that Damien is engaged, there's no reason to hold on to the hope of being with him one day. It's time for me to take a deep breath, pull up my big girl panties and move on.

Drinks Friday night sound perfect. "Just what the doctor ordered."

"Table for two?" The waitress rolls her eyes as she takes in Laney's outfit. The girl can't help herself. She's self-confident, wearing loud colors and short skirts. Her spikey hair always looks like she just rolled out of bed but I know she spends hours on it. She pierced her nose last week and it's her. I can't even remember what she looked like without it. I envy her.

She's fierce and exactly what I strive to be.

"Did you see her roll her eyes at me?" She laughs as she pulls out her barstool. "What a bitch."

"Jealousy. That's all it is." I wink at the bartender as he approaches us. "Two chocolate martinis please."

"So spill it." Laney applies another layer of lip gloss and licks her lips. Her eyes never leave the bartender. "I love a man covered in tattoos. If I lick him, he's mine."

I can't help but stare as he puts down our drinks and she leans across the bar and licks his neck. Fearless. I'm going to start making mental notes. By the end of the night, I will be a flirting pro. "You're a rock star. I swear you have no filter and no fear.

Teach me oh wise one. I need to learn your wild ways."

"Says the woman being screwed by the lead singer of Liquid Regret."

"It wasn't like that. It was sweet and innocent. A little romantic. It was never more than that." I wring my hands together in my lap. "I knew he was leaving and I tried to protect myself. I fell in love with him and I let him walk away. I never did anything to pursue him. Now he's getting married and I'm spending my Friday night in a bar with you. So, cheers."

Laney's eyes grow wide as she stares behind me. I don't even want to know what her next prey looks like. It will just further depress me and remind me that I have no social skills whatsoever. I take another sip of my drink waiting for her to say something but nothing comes. The hair on the back of my neck stands up and my stomach churns. I don't even need to turn around to know who will be there. Taking a deep breath, I bite my lip and watch Laney for clues. When she stands up and walks away, I have my answer. He's here.

"Mia." He whispers.

Chapter 3

"Silence is my enemy, the demon that
haunts me.
You've stolen my soul, I will never be
free." – Liquid Regret

Holy shit. She's here. I know it the second I walk into this hole in the wall bar. She's sitting with her back to me but I would recognize her anywhere. The expression on her friend's face is priceless. I pray that she isn't about to scream or rush me. I just want a night off from the bullshit. The rumor about my engagement is ridiculous but I don't see any way out of it. I beat myself up all day and complained so much that I thought the guys would throw me off the tour bus. It's my new reality, like it or not.

I stop dead in my tracks when I hear her voice. She's telling her friend about us. My heart swells with pride. The object of every wet dream I've had, the vision I see every night when I go to bed, the muse for every lyric I have written for months. And she's right here. If I reach my hand out, I'll touch that perfect, pale skin.

"Mia." I whisper her name and she tenses. I smile at the goose bumps that break out on her arms.

She turns slowly, her emerald eyes wide with shock. "Damien." Her voice is breathless. I immediately want to wrap my arms around her. "What are you doing here?"

Do I hug her? I'm not sure. Fuck it. I pull her into my chest, burying my nose in her hair. Every nerve ending in my body is instantly alive. This girl is an obsession. Her arms are slow to close around my waist, but when they do, I'm home. I've instantly forgotten about my shitty session with the band today. My pretend engagement to that supermodel witch is stripped from my memory. There is nothing in this moment but Mia and how my life is better with her near me.

She pulls away quickly and I stumble backwards. Her eyes are wide and moist. "We have a week off before we hit the West Coast. The guys call this home so here we are. Why are you here?"

Her smile doesn't reach her eyes. "I moved here a while back. I got a job offer and I wanted to be closer to Lil."

"You look beautiful." Her hair is longer and her eyes seem brighter.

"Dude." Harley laughs behind me. "D's a rude son of a bitch. Hi. I'm Harley."

Mia laughs and takes his hand. I should have known Harley wouldn't shake it. Bastard kisses her hand and winks. "I'm Mia."

"Oh Shit. The legendary Mia?" Lennon about crawls over Harley to get to her. "Nice to meet you, sweetness. I'm Chance. As in, want to take a chance on me?"

"Jesus. Back the fuck off." I can't help but laugh. They've heard the stories, pulled me out of my own ass when I needed it and now, they are meeting the woman that sent my brain into a tailspin. "They're cavemen. Ignore them. They don't get out much."

Mia's laugh is musical. "It's nice to meet you guys. I'm a huge fan."

"Please. We're the fans. We're happy to meet the woman who's inspired some of D's best lyrics."

She blushes and it's the most beautiful fucking thing I've ever seen. She is the definition of pretty. No matter how many nights are spent thinking about her, the real thing doesn't even compare. How in the hell did I walk away from this? I am certain of exactly one thing in this world. I will not walk away again.

Mia's friend walks back to the table, smile on her face and her chest poked out to the heavens. It's wasted on me. I can't see past the redhead who is laughing next to her. "This is my friend, Laney."

Without saying a word, Laney walks up to Harley and licks his neck. "If I lick it, it's mine." The whole table erupts in laughter.

"Sorry, kiddo. Harley here has a wife. Lucky for you, I'm available. Lick away." Chance throws his arm around Laney and leads her back up to the bar.

"Want to take a walk?" I need to get her out of this bar. I need to get her somewhere that isn't filled with prying eyes and assholes with cameras. The highest bidder doesn't need pictures of me tonight. "Get some fresh air?"

She looks around, suddenly nervous. "That probably isn't the best idea. Oksana probably wouldn't appreciate that. I know I wouldn't if I were in her shoes."

"Mia. It's not like that."

"I'm pretty sure it is. You're engaged and that means that the only walking I need to be doing with you is walking away." She grabs her purse, gives Laney a quick wave and takes a deep breath. "I know this will probably sound stupid, but it took me a long time to get up in the morning and not miss you so much. I have a simple life here and I want to keep it that way."

"Mia." I grab her hand, stopping her from leaving. "I can't explain it all to you. It won't make any sense but it's all about image and publicity. It's all an illusion to help me out of the shit hole I put myself into. Please don't leave. Give me a few minutes."

When she bites her bottom lip, I'm a goner. I want to sink my teeth into it. I'm absolutely whipped and all I've done is kiss this girl. "Everything in me is screaming to stay except my heart. It's saying run and I need to listen to it."

She leans into me, hugs me gently and pulls away. Her eyes tell me the whole story. The girl is just as screwed as I am. Maybe a little time will bring her around but one thing is certain, this is not the last I will see of Mia Lee on this break. Nope. I will camp out on her front porch if I have to. Before I get back on that tour bus, she's mine.

"Get your head out of your ass, Reynolds." Max is screaming at me from behind his drum kit. I'm about three seconds away from kicking his ass. He thinks he's safe back there behind his big drums but I'm not above crawling over them and choking him. "Reynolds, what the fuck, man?"

"Stop."   When Harley stops playing his guitar, it's serious. "Whatever it is that has your head fucked up, fix it. You're missing the harmony completely.   You've forgotten the words twice and they're your lyrics. Let's take five."

This is the worst I've ever been. It's practice but it doesn't mean I can blow it off like it's nothing. They're right. My head is all over the place. The one place it isn't is here in the studio.

"We need to get these tracks laid tonight. Chance and I will do that. Go home and get some sleep. We record tomorrow. Pay attention to the bridge on Stolen Soul. You're flat and it sounds like shit. Seymour thinks this is our next breakout song. You feel me?"

The death gaze Harley gives me is enough to get me to stop and pay attention. "Sorry about today, guys. I have a lot on my mind. I'll get my shit straight before tomorrow."

"I know this engagement is bullshit. She's a bitch and the last few times I saw her, she was strung out and whining about everything in life. You need to look at how you got here, man. Trust Joshua. He's got your best interest at heart. He's trying to make sense out of this downward spiral you've been in. Play the game for now. I don't see any other way. Do you?" Harley shrugs his shoulders and looks back at his guitar. "We all fuck up. Look at us. We're the definition of dysfunctional. But you made your bed, lie in it and get comfy."

"Oh wise one." Chance bows at him.

"Get the fuck out of here." Harley laughs and points at the door.

I don't need to be told twice. The hotel room is calling my name. I need a good night of rest, a hot shower and a little perspective. I'm home for a week. I'll give her another day. Maybe I can convince her to come to the show on Sunday night. I know I have to be careful. Mia has the potential to blow Joshua's cover up out of the water. That could be detrimental to my career. And it's not just about me anymore. I have three other people that are living this dream along with me. They're counting on me to do the right thing and if I fuck it up, I'm screwing over my family. It's my own fault. I couldn't keep it in my pants. Thank God no one has noticed that the countless, faceless women that have been along for the ride the last year all look like Mia.

"Shit."

Chapter 4

The morning sun streams in my bedroom window, bringing with it the promise of a new day. I love my apartment. It's tiny and on the outskirts of the city but the rent is low and the neighbors are friendly. I'm on the tenth floor and my view is amazing. It is a diamond in the rough and I'm blessed that I found it.

Most of the world is still asleep at this hour on a Saturday. It's my favorite time to run and let go of my stress. It's always been my time. My brain shuts off and I concentrate on the sound of my breathing. It is my sanctuary when life gets hard.

Last night was a reality check. Seeing Damien again made my heart race.   Running into him was unexpected and it had been a test. I could have given into my heart and jumped at the chance to be alone with him.   Every part of my body was screaming at me to hold him, to spend one more night with him. I've spent the last year ignoring the voice in my head that told me I love him.   Last night, I realized it was right.

I don't know what I'm supposed to do with this knowledge. The only thing I do know is that I have to stay away from him. Before I know it, he'll be back on the road with the band and last night will be a distant memory.

Stretching my arms above my head, my mind wanders back to our last morning together.   We hadn't slept at all the night before.   We'd stayed up all night laughing. He's the funniest person I've ever met and it was so easy to get lost in him with just a smile. He was the missing piece in the puzzle that was my life. He was exactly what I needed, exactly when I needed him.

We'd spent a week together. We'd gone to the movies and cooked dinner together. We'd been your everyday couple despite his rock star status. We held hands on the couch while we watched TV. We laughed constantly. He knew what I was thinking before I ever said anything.

Our chemistry was off the charts. When he kissed me, my toes curled. My body craved him. His hands were magic and made me feel things I'd never felt. He made my body respond in ways it hadn't before. We'd promised to take things slowly and even though we almost crossed the line more than a few times, he respected me enough not to push for more.

When the sun finally made its appearance that morning, the reality of his leaving hit me hard. We spent our last hour just lying in bed staring at each other. His touch was so gentle and his eyes so full of passion. I wanted to give myself to him but I wasn't sure my heart would survive it. Tears fell from my eyes but the silence between us spoke volumes. He wiped my tears away and held me until the last second. When it was time, he kissed me on the cheek and told me it had been the best time of his whole life.

I need to get out of this apartment. I feel like the walls are closing in on me. I need to feel the sun on my face and the pavement under my feet. I pull on my yoga pants and tank, then throw my hair into a messy pony tail. I need to hit the streets before the world wakes up.

The hallway to the elevator always smells like beer. It's the only downside to living here. The college age girls down the hall love having people over. I never hear them but I can always smell the remnants of last night's party. They invite me every Friday. Maybe I should go. They are a few years younger than I am but they all seem pretty nice. I need to get out more.

The elevator ding snaps me back to reality. When the doors open, I freeze. This can't be happening. He looks up from his phone and his eyes widen. His smile brightens his entire face. Damn him for being in my space again.

"Mia." He takes a step forward but my hand stops him. He backs up and lets me in.

"You can talk to me on the way down. I have somewhere I need to be and I don't have much time." My hands are shaking. Traitors.

"I'll take whatever time you're willing to give me." Damien presses the first floor button.

This may be the longest elevator ride in history. Shit, he smells amazing. "What do you want, Damien? I meant what I said last night. We can't spend time together. It's too hard for me."

His grip is firm as he grabs my arm. I've missed his touch. My hurt is mirrored back in his eyes. I'm not blind. I know he has feelings for me. But I refuse to be the other woman in anyone's life. My parents are happily married, my sister is getting married and I don't see their marriage lasting any less than fifty years or so. I want forever. I want loyalty. And above all, I want someone that loves me with his whole heart. Damien is engaged. He is not my forever. Repeat that all day, brain.

The elevator moans and stops. The lights flicker and I gasp. I pound the button for the first floor. Nothing happens. "Oh my God." I'm panicking. I can't stand being stuck in a small space. Thoughts of plummeting to my death take over. Cue the panic attack.

Damien puts his hands on my cheeks. "Breathe. It's ok. I'm here with you. It's just a power outage or something. You're safe." His chuckle makes me furious. "Baby, you need to breathe."

"Breathe? We're about the fall to our deaths. This thing is a death trap. I'm going to die in this elevator that reeks of beer and will soon be splattered with my blood. There's no way to avoid this. I used to think if you jumped right before you crashed to the ground, that might help break the impact but I realized the ceiling would crush me into a thousand useless pieces. If I climb out the door at the top, I'll just be free falling when this thing lets loose."

Damien's laugh gets louder. "Christ. You've given this some thought."

I'm in full panic mode. "I can't breathe. It's hot in here. Are you hot?

I'm on fire. I think I'm having a heart attack. Oh my God." I gasp for air.

"Mia." Damien shakes me. "Look at me. Concentrate on me. That's my girl. Deep breath. Good. Look into my eyes."

His voice soothes my soul. His hands run up and down my arms and my body begins to relax. I hate small spaces, I hate elevators, I hate not being in control. "I'm scared." My voice is weak. It's not a voice I recognize. My body trembles. I'm terrified.

"You're ok. Sit with me. I'll sing some of the new lyrics I'm working on and maybe you can help me figure out what's missing. Can you do that for me?"

I have to give him credit. He's trying to keep me calm. "I'd love that."

He clears his throat as he sits down next to me. "It's rough but I think it'll be really good when we're done. Ready?" I nod my head and he smiles. His soulful voice fills the elevator.

'I got drunk off your touch and high off your kiss. The taste of your lips I forever will miss. You've ruined me. I'm broken. You've ruined me. I'm lost. You've ruined me.'

My mouth hangs open. When he sings, the world stops. His words are beautiful and I can't take my eyes off him. I can't help myself. His voice transports me to another place. I am completely healed. My anxiety is gone. The elevator is no longer my enemy. It's just a reason to be near him and I'm suddenly thankful that we're stuck.

"Damien, that was..." I struggle to find the words. "It was beautiful. I can't wait to hear that with the band behind you. It's almost haunting."

"You haunt me." His hand reaches for me. I want to pull away but I can't. His fingers trace my lips. "I wrote that the day I left Georgia. I've thought about you every day since."

"Damien."

He cuts me off. "Mia, I've made more mistakes that I can even count. I thought if I found someone else, I could get over you. Every night was a mistake bigger than the last. Everything reminded me of you. I got totally lost. I completely fucked up."

I shake my head. "You can't say this to me. You can't. It'll break me."

"I need you to know everything. Please." His eyes widen as he starts to confess. "The guys couldn't stop the bullshit that got deeper every time we stopped in a new city. I knew I was fucking up but I couldn't stop. I needed anything to numb me. The women were just stand-ins. All of them. Oskana included. She's somebody I met in one of the cities. Her manager is a friend of Joshua's. Her career was heading into the toilet and we did some appearances together. There's nothing there. She's a cover up story for all the bullshit I started. The label wanted my image cleaned up and Joshua came up with this fucking story that I don't know how to get out of."

I can't stop the tears. I don't even want to. Damien is broken and I love him. I have for so long. I wish things were easy. Just for once. Our lives are too different. I would give up almost anything to make his pain go away. Our love story was over a lifetime ago but I can't help but wonder if I had stopped him that morning, if I had begged him to stay in my life, would he have taken a chance on us? Would his story be completely different now? Would my heart still be shattered into a million pieces?

Chapter 5

Drowning, I'm told, is a bad way to die.
Yet, you killed my soul with a simple
goodbye. I'm drowning in you. –
Liquid Regret

She's crying and I feel like my heart is being ripped from my chest. She's honestly the most beautiful woman I've ever seen. I shouldn't have been such a fuck up. How different would things be if I hadn't thought with my dick every night on the road? I need to stop being such a pussy. Joshua needs to know this cover up bullshit doesn't work for me. I want Mia, consequences be damned.

"Please don't cry." I wipe the tears from her cheeks. I'll make any excuse to touch her. I'm weak. "I'm sorry for everything. I know that's not enough. I walked away like an asshole."

"No you didn't." She looks down at her lap. "We were both stupid. I believe in the white horse fairytale and the power of destiny. If I'd been thinking like an adult, I would have gotten your number and used the tickets."

"So, take it now." I grab her cell phone and dial my number. When my phone rings, I smile. I now have Mia's number and I plan on using it. A lot. "I never pushed you. I won't start now. But I want to see you, Mia. I want to have a reason to rush back to LA after a few weeks on the road."

"What about Oksana? How bad will it be if they find out that was all a lie?" Even after I'm a screw up, she worries about me.

"I don't know. I need to talk to Josh. But first, I want to do this."

I move slowly. I don't want her to pull away. I can see her heartbeat pick up in her neck. Her breathing changes and I know she's right here with me. I take her face in my hands, tilting her head back and brushing my lips across hers. The kiss is gentle and I wait for her to react. Her moan against my lips tells me everything I need to know. My whole body is on high alert.

She melts into me, letting me pull her closer. Her lips part and I need to be inside her. My tongue glides into her mouth, dancing with hers like they were made for each other. Her fingers tangle into my hair. Everything in my life fades away. It's only Mia. Nothing else exists. In this minute, I'm a complete person.

She tugs at my shirt, pulling it from my jeans. My brain is in overdrive. Her hands trail up my abdomen, resting on my pecs, digging her nails into my skin. Her breathing is ragged. I need a minute to think. I pull out of the kiss, trailing my tongue down her neck, inhaling her scent. The air is thick with arousal and I am ready to tear her clothes off. I'm hard as a rock and I can't form any coherent thought.

Her foot runs up my leg and that's my opening. I pick her up, her perfect ass in my hands. I'm in heaven. I push her against the wall of the elevator, holding her up with my weight, feeling her legs wrap around me. I grind my erection against her and she gasps. Her yoga pants leave very little to the imagination. I push against her again and she bites my lip. Shit. This is going to escalate quickly and that's exactly what I want. My brain is screaming at me to take her, mark my territory, and prove to her that no one else can make her feel the way I can.

In all our time together, we've never gotten this far. I know it's too fast. I know it isn't the time or the place to get lost in each other. I can feel her heat. It's pouring off of her. Her cheeks are flushed. She rubs against me and moans. Her legs are shaking. I want to know what she feels like. I want to know what she looks like when she shatters apart. I want to hear her moan my name when she explodes in ecstasy.

"Wait." She's breathless. Her hands still and she rests her head on my shoulder. "I need a minute."

I run my hands in circles on her back. My heart is pounding out of my chest. This woman is going to be the death of me. I'm going to have a chronic case of blue balls and it might kill me. She's worth the painful death. She's worth the wait. I know that with all my heart. I just need to clue Damien junior in. He's going to be pissed when he gets the news. He's desperate for her body.

She jumps away from me and it scares the shit out of me. "What are we doing? I'm sorry." She's covering her mouth and shaking her head. I cannot let her run.

"Don't say you're sorry. Say anything but not that you're sorry it happened. Nothing that feels that right is wrong. It can't be."

The lights flicker on and the elevator moans back to life. Fuck. My window of opportunity is over. I need to think of something, anything that will keep her talking. She grabs her phone and I would give anything to know what she's thinking.

"Mia, what if I talk to Joshua? He's not unreasonable. I know he had my best interest in mind when he leaked the story. He's not just my manager. He's a good friend. He'll understand."

She takes a deep breath. "Let's say he does. And he retracts the story. Then what? What kind of fall out will that have for the band? I couldn't live with knowing that I'm ruining lives. What about your son?"

I smile at the thought of Xander. "He's thirteen. He's not completely naïve. He knows who you are and he knows that I screwed up. I think it would teach him that you shouldn't give up on what you really want."

Xander and I have spent a lot of time emailing the past week. He's grown into a young man and I've missed it. He's got his first girlfriend and they hang out at the mall. He claims he's in love with her. I know he is in his own way. But it's nothing like what I feel for Mia. It's my job to teach him about life, disappointments and all. He's watched my downfall through the media and through whatever lies or stories he's been told from those that aren't my biggest fans. He knows about Mia and that I have spiraled out of control because I let go of something that could be everything to me. Teaching him to fight for love is a lesson he needs to learn. I wish someone had taught me that lesson.

"I just need time to process all this. I don't want to get hurt any more than I already have been. I know it's my fault. I swear I'm my own worst enemy. I just don't want to jump in if I don't know what's going to be there when I land. I'm scared."

The elevator doors slide open, bringing with it the fear of the unknown. "Mia, you never know what's out there if you don't take a chance. The biggest successes in life are because someone took a leap into the unknown. It's the fear that makes it exciting. It's the belief that makes it great."

"D Rey in the house." Joshua chuckles as I trip on the step leading into the studio. I can't do anything but shoot him the bird and watch as my bandmates laugh.

"On time and with a shit eating grin on his face. Looks like some sleep did you good." Harley nods before looking back down at his music. He's the serious one of the group but I feel closer to him than I ever have to my family.

"Or he got laid." Max raises his eyebrows and starts laughing. "You did, you dirty son of a bitch."

"Jesus Christ. Please tell me no one saw you. This story blows up in our faces and we're done." Joshua is on his feet before I can say anything.

"I didn't get laid and there aren't any pictures so sit back down before the aneurysm ruptures. You are wound way too fucking tight, man." I don't like the look he's giving me. I've known him long enough to know that he can read me like a book. He sees right through all the bullshit. "Seriously, it's cool."

"Let's do this. We have the studio for three hours. Let's lay down some tracks so we can concentrate on the show tomorrow."

I'd been completely delusional when I thought I would lead this band of misfits. Harley has this shit locked down and I can't imagine it any other way. He's our lead guitarist, our faithful leader, the voice of the group and everyone's conscience. I know I've let him down the past year. I worked hard but I fucked harder. Everything I did during the day brought me to what I really wanted at night. But Harley never questioned me. He and Della stood by my side every second.

Della. She's like my sister. All those years chasing our dreams, living in shit holes, moving from place to place, running down something we weren't sure we'd ever catch. And there she was, running right alongside us. She's the real rock star. She's our biggest cheerleader, even if the accomplishment is a small one. What she and Harley have is exactly what I want. I can only picture that with one person.

"I want to record 'Ruin' first. I know we decided on 'Stolen Soul' but I lose myself in 'Ruin'. I feel it, I breathe it. If we're here to record our next big song, I don't want it to be anything else."

I hold my breath and look at Harley. His lips twitch as he tries not to smile. The bastard is going to let Joshua scream and throw a tantrum before he agrees with me. I deserve it. I brace myself as Josh stands up from the soundboard. This is going to be a shit storm that I should have braced myself for.

He stops right in front of me, his breath hot on my face. "Then get your fucking ass in there and create a masterpiece."

Chapter 6

It's been a full day and I can still feel him on my lips. I can still feel his strong hands tangled in my hair. The look of pure ecstasy on his face when I rubbed my body against his is forever seared into my memory. Every thought in my brain is telling me to run. But my heart, my traitorous heart that can't beat without him, has taken control. Tonight I'm going to tell him that I want a chance. There's safety in knowing he feels exactly the same way. His text messages told me what I wanted to hear. The flowers sitting on my kitchen table are proof that this man is it for me.

I dress quickly. The concert starts in just a few hours and my sister and her fiancé are meeting me there. I know Damien loves my hair down so I spent extra time curling it and getting it to flow down my back like it was effortless. The girl staring at me in the mirror is someone I haven't seen for a year. She's smiling, her eyes are bright, there's excitement surrounding her. That's the me I remember. I'm happy to see this girl again.

The late afternoon breeze feels like heaven. The sun is still shining but the extreme heat of the summer is fading. The waves roll In the background, calming my nerves. The beach is packed with surfers and sun worshipers. Music blankets the air. Los Angeles is beautiful. This is the first time I've seen it through these eyes. I'm happy. I can't help but giggle as I step into the limo that Damien sent to pick me up.

The butterflies take flight as soon as the car rolls forward. My nerves are in complete control for a minute and I need to calm down. I wonder if he's spoken to his manager about us. I asked him to give me a little time to think. Part of me is hoping he hasn't said anything yet. I'd like to be there when he does. I need Joshua to see that I'm serious about this. I need him to see how much Damien means to me.

This is the perfect night for an outdoor concert. As we pull up to the Hollywood Bowl, I see Steve and Lily waiting for me. I have to take a few calming breaths before I step out into the real world. They know I've seen Damien but that's all they know. I don't have much else to report.

They'll both be happy for me so I don't fully understand my hesitation. I guess if I admit it to myself, then it becomes real. As soon as we go public, my life will have no privacy. No quiet. No peace.

"You look gorgeous, kiddo." Steve greets me with his usual hug and kiss on the head. I couldn't have picked someone more perfect for my sister. If I had created someone with everything she deserved all in one package, it would've been Steve Wainwright, hands down.

"Hi." I smile when he eyes the limo and gives me that familiar big brother eyebrow raise.

"New wheels?" His smirk is adorable.

"What? Did you drive here yourselves? Lil, he doesn't think you deserve a limo?" I giggle as I hug my sister.

"Hey, I bought her Moretti's house. She's lucky I didn't drive her here on the back of a moped." Lily hits Steve's arm. They're so in love. It makes me gag. It also makes me insanely jealous.

"Damien has us set up with backstage passes. Let's head back before the show starts. I can't wait to see his ugly mug." Steve pulls us both through the crowd to the back entrance. He smiles as he shows security his tickets.

The guy standing guard in back looks like one of those crazy guys that pulls airplanes in those strong man competitions. He's enormous, bald and dressed head to toe in black. There is no way in hell that I would ever mess with him. When he meets my eyes, there's no emotion in his at all. I smile. I feel a little better knowing someone so menacing is guarding what's so important to me. He nods slightly. I may have imagined it. Either way, I'm happy he's here.

"Seymour, I've got three people out here that say they're guests of D's. Want me to send them back? Or hold them here?" He talks into his headset.

I can't help but fidget. This will be the first time I'll meet the legendary Joshua Seymour. I've heard stories and imagine him to be as daunting as Mr. Personality here holding us back from the stage.

Steve's face is grim. "Is all this security really necessary? It's a band, not the president."

"You'd be surprised by all the crazy shit that goes down at these things. We've had to up our security detail since Harley started getting threats." Mr. Biceps actually looks worried for a minute.

"Threats?" Lily leans into Steve.

My heart is pounding. I haven't heard anything about this. I imagine their life on the road is pretty crazy. I know women throw themselves at them everywhere they go. I know cameras follow them, the highest bidder getting the best shot. I've never given much thought to anything more than that. My stomach churns. Have people threatened Damien? My palms are suddenly sweating.

A blond man dressed in khakis and a dress shirt steps out from the hallway and smiles at Mr. Muscles. He doesn't look much older than Damien. His sleeves are rolled up, displaying a Rolex covered in diamonds. The thing has to be worth more than my car and everything I own in my apartment. He smiles and his face softens. Dimples dip in his cheeks. His face is spattered with freckles. He looks like one of the guys Steve hangs out with. The tall one that's married to the doctor. Their names have completely escaped me.

He extends his hand to Steve. "You must be Steve. The resemblance is pretty astounding. I'm Joshua Seymour."

"Nice to meet you." Steve shakes his hand. "This is my fiancé, Lily and her sister, Mia."

Joshua freezes. His eyes roam over me, finally settling on my face. His face pales. For just one second, he loses his composure. I feel like I'm going to lose my dinner. "It's very nice to meet you. The band is back here warming up. They usually zone out right before a show. I'll take you back so you can say hello before they go on."

Backstage is crazy. There are people everywhere. The opening act is doing a sound check and the lighting and sound crews are frantic. The excitement buzzes through my veins. I'm standing in the center of Damien's world. I'm getting a glimpse of his life that I haven't seen before. It's an adrenaline rush. The nerves leave my body and are replaced with joy.

Damien looks up as I walk in. Holy shit. The man is a god. His ripped jeans hug his hips like they were made for his body. His white tee is almost painted on, showing his six pack underneath. I can't breathe as he walks toward me. His smile is blinding. I'm a goner. How I ever thought I could stay away from this man is beyond me. He's beautiful. Sex appeal rolls off his shoulders.

"Mia." He whispers in my ear as he hugs me. His voice caresses me. "You are so fucking beautiful."

He pulls away from me and our eyes lock. His remind me of the ocean. They're the brightest aqua I've ever seen. The electricity sparks between us. The rest of the room has disappeared and we're alone. This minute is just for us. His hands cup my face and he leans in. My body moves on its own accord, meeting him halfway, melting into him. Sparks explode behind my eyes every time our lips touch. It's powerful and intimate. I'm lost to him. Our tongues meet and he deepens the kiss. His hands tangle in my hair, holding me impossibly close. There isn't an inch between us. I want more. I want it now, right here. Fear be damned.

A throat clears and we jump apart. "What the fuck is this?" Joshua's face is red and his hands are balled into fists.

"Josh, this is Mia. My Mia." Damien puts his arm around my shoulder.

"Fuck." He starts to pace. "Don't be stupid, Damien. We'll talk about this later."

"There's really nothing to talk about." He kisses my temple.

"What about Oksana?" Josh is rubbing his temples.

"I don't give a shit about her. You know that, Josh."

"You told me to spin this story. Think long and hard before you do something stupid.   You're three seconds away from being dropped by the label.   Don't fuck this up for everyone."

"Stop." Harley puts his hand up and all eyes turn to him. "The label drops him, they drop us all. They'd be completely stupid to do that. We see the jets and the cars. We bought those for them. No way will they give that up. We've got a show in a few and we need to focus. Josh, show our guests to their seats.   We'll talk tomorrow."

Damien smiles at me. "I'll see you after the show. Meet me in my dressing room."

I just nod. It won't be long until he's back out on the road. Tonight, he's mine.

Chapter 7

Fear suffocates me, I can't take a breath
The last glimpse of light, the moment of death – Liquid Regret

The crowd is alive. The screaming sends an adrenaline rush through my veins. It's the same high I used to get when I would shoot up. If I'm honest with myself, I've replaced one addiction with another my whole life. It's probably the reason I continue to cover my body in tattoos. Sure, I love the art. But it covers my scars. The darkest time in my life.

The lights go dark. I listen to the screams. It's heaven. I was born for this. Max is pounding on his drums. Encore number two. I never dreamed it would be like this. We've saved our most popular song for last. Without Novocain starts and the crowd goes crazy. My voice is scratchy now. The two hours on stage have taken their toll.

I can see Mia in the front row. She's staring, wide eyed. Tonight will be different. No lines of women for me tonight. Or any other night. I'd trade my left nut to be buried deep in her gorgeous body. I won't push her. Jesus, I hope she wants me too. Only another two minutes until I leave this stage and head to my dressing room. There will be no meet and greet. The only meeting I'm having is with Mia. Clothing optional.

When the song ends, we're rushed off stage. The security detail flanks Harley, keeping him separated from the crowd. The last few months have been crazy. I used to joke about wanting a stalker. It's not funny anymore. It's fucking scary. Some bitch has latched onto him and is just crazy enough to try some bullshit. It started simply enough. Cards, notes, the occasional gift. Nothing was signed but we knew they were all from her. The same words, the same perfume. A few weeks later, Della had to call the police in the middle of the night. Someone tried to get in their house and left the backdoor open when they left. Josh upped the security detail at their house. The security system was upgraded. Everything is being done to keep Harley safe. People are fucking crazy.

I throw myself on the couch in my dressing room, chugging a bottle of water. The heat onstage is intense. I'm covered in sweat so I take my shirt off. I need to cool off before Mia shows up. Thoughts of her make my heart speed up. I'm completely pussy whipped.

I have no concept of time when I'm on stage. Everything is blocked by song and set. I just sing until they tell me to stop. It's an intense work out and I leave exhausted and fulfilled. I miss being out there every night but the break is nice. It's not long before we hit the road again. Twenty more cities. Then I'll have to get my shit together. I'll find a house and settle down. I'll get joint custody of Xander for the months we aren't on tour. I'll be normal. And I can concentrate on a relationship with Mia without all the hype of the paparazzi. It'll be nice to wake up in the morning and know Josh isn't going to be banging on my hotel room door.

I jump when a hand touches my chest. I didn't hear her come in. Fuck. Her hair is windblown, her cheeks pink from the breeze. Her eyes are bright and excited. She sees through all the layers of shit and can see the real me. She could bring me to my knees with a simple smile.

"You were amazing." She straddles my lap. The minute I feel her heat, I'm hard. "Damien the rock star is hot."

I'd laugh but I'm afraid to move. She's never been this aggressive and I don't want her to stop. Her chest rubs against mine and she licks my neck. One long smooth stroke. Her hands run up my arms and stop at my shoulders. I shiver. She smirks. She knows she's got me. Right now, I'm totally ok with that. She rolls her hips, rubbing against my cock. Holy shit.

My hands instinctively move to her hips, guiding her against me. She bites her lip and tips her head back. Her breathing is short and choppy. This feels too good. I need more.

"Mia." She shakes her head, stopping me from saying any more. Her lips crash against mine, claiming my mouth. Her tongue is aggressive, owning me. I feel the button on my jeans give way before I realize what she's doing. Her hand slides into the waist band of my boxers. I tense for just a second. She's not like the others. She isn't here because I'm a rock star. She's here because I'm Damien. All my fear is wiped away as she cups my hard shaft. I gasp. Her hand is like fire. I've wanted this forever. "Shit."

"Is this ok?" She's blushing. Her eyes are wide as she waits for my answer.

"Fuck, yes it's ok." I push her hair back, tangling it in my hands and pulling her into me. "I've wanted you forever."

"Then take me." Her hips grind against me. If she keeps this up, it won't last long. I need to take control.

I flip her onto her back, pulling her to the edge of the couch. Her dress makes it easy for me to get to what I want. Her black, lace thong against her pale skin takes my breath away. I dip a finger between her folds and she's soaked. I need to be inside her. I need it more than I need to breathe.

"Are you sure?" If she says no, my balls are going to explode. My fingers graze her clit and she moans. Fuck.

"I've never been this sure of anything. Stop talking and make love to me." She reaches for my erection, wrapping her hand around it and pulling once, twice. Shit.

I have to taste her. I pull her panties to the side and lick up her lips, ending at her clit with a circle. She cries out. I suck her hardened nub into my teeth and bite it lightly. Her body jolts at the sensation. I've never cared about my partner getting off. I'm a selfish son of a bitch. But Mia's different and I need her to come. I need her to come a lot.

"That feels so good." She grabs my hair and pulls. I'll take all my cues from her. I need to know every inch of her body. I pull her clit between my teeth again and she throws her head back, slamming her eyes closed.

"No way, baby. Eyes on me." Her emerald eyes lock with mine and I flick my tongue against her, speeding up with every lick. Her legs begin to shake. She bites her lip and tries to pull away. Not a chance. She's close. I whisper to her, my voice rough from the show. "Let go, Mia."

I slide one finger into her, pressing on the spot I know will make her shatter. My tongue continues its assault. She gasps, grabbing at the cushions on the couch. Her nails dig into the fabric and she screams. Her taste explodes in my mouth. It's the most amazing thing I've ever tasted. I'll never get enough of her.

"Please. I need you." She's breathless, her hair splayed on the cushions like a halo. She's pulling on my clothes, almost desperate. She's not alone. I need to be buried deep. I need to feel her wrapped around me. Now that I've had a taste, I need more. I need it all.

I pull a condom from my bag and pull my jeans off. She doesn't move, just watches me. Her eyes burn into me. I would die for this woman. She has no idea what she does to me.

"Let me." She sits up and takes the condom from me. It might be the longest minute of my life. I'm hyperaware of everything. The tear of the wrapper, her hands on me, the heat of her gaze. She rolls it on, taking more time than I can stand. She giggles when I growl.

Once it's on, I'm ready to attack. Mia has other plans. She stands and pushes me onto the couch. She reaches behind her, untying the string keeping her dress at her shoulders. It falls to her waist. She's not wearing a bra. Jesus, she's the most beautiful woman I have ever seen. Her breasts are perfect. They're enough for my hands, perky, pink. Her nipples stand at attention. I want to sink my teeth into them.

Sounds from the dressing room next door hardly register as she comes closer to me. Her eyes widen and she looks behind me at the wall. She laughs and covers her mouth. I shake myself out of the Mia trance I'm in. The moans next door get louder and a female voice yells out Chance's name. I want to kill him. I'm terrified Mia will run. Instead, she looks at me with a devious grin and straddles my lap.

"That's a huge turn on." She kisses my neck and listens to the screams of passion next door. "But I think we can do better."

Without any kind of warning, she slides down my shaft, taking all of me in one stroke. I see stars. She's hot. Her walls squeeze me. When she begins to move, I think I may die of pleasure. She grabs her nipples as she bounces up and down on my cock. She's wet and the sound echoes around the dressing room. I can't stand this slow torture. I need it fast. I need to hear her scream as I pound into her.

I grab her hips, stilling her above me. Her hooded eyes meet mine. I slide down to get better footing. It's my turn. I pick up the pace, moving in and out as quickly as I can without losing my mind. She starts to moan. It's the most erotic sound I've ever heard.

"More." Her head falls back, her mouth open in ecstasy.

I stand, our bodies still attached and carry her to the vanity. I set her down and kiss her with everything I've got. I've never loved anyone before. I imagine this is how it feels. I'll scare the shit out of her if I tell her.

She leans forward and bites my shoulder, pulling me out of my day dream. I look at her and I know she knows. My strokes are long and slow. She leans against the lighted mirror. She wraps her legs around me, deepening my strokes. My body rubs against her clit and she starts to pant. Making her come is my new favorite thing to do.

"I'm so close," she whispers, as she digs her nails into my arms. "Make me come, Damien."

Challenge accepted. I pull her legs up, over my shoulders. I slam into her and she screams. I put my thumb on her clit. I can feel her pulse. She's swollen and ready. "Ready?" I ask her, smiling as she can't answer me. I pinch the sensitive bundle of nerves and she detonates. Her orgasm rushes from her, covering my shaft, running down my legs. It's the hottest fucking thing I've ever seen.

"Damien!" She screams my name. I've never heard anything more fucking sexy.

Chapter 8

I've never felt anything like this. Every stroke brings me closer to orgasm. I've already had one. I've never believed in multiple orgasms. Damien is proving me wrong.

I can hear how wet I am. I can hear Chance next door having sex. It's so erotic. It brings me that much closer to coming. This feels so good. We fit together perfectly. His pace is frantic and he rubs against my clit with each stroke.

I dig my nails into his arms and he looks at me. His aqua eyes see right into my heart. He's gorgeous. He smiles and I can't talk. I'm so close. Warmth begins to spread through my belly. He's hitting my g spot, he's touching my clit, he's too much.

My legs shake and I can't stop them. The most powerful orgasm I've ever had rips from my body. Light sparks behind my eyes. I scream his name so loud and I don't care. His pace never slows. He just stares at me, eyes hooded and gorgeous, and pumps into me so hard I don't ever want him to stop.

I could look at him forever. His tattooed body, the stubble on his chin, the eyes that bring me to my knees. He's everything. I fell for him over a year ago. The feelings are even stronger now. He notices I'm staring and winks. He pulls my face toward him, holding my cheeks and rubbing his thumbs against my skin. It's an intimate gesture and my heart pounds.

"Nothing has ever felt this good." He's winded and sweating. He's delicious. "I don't want this to end."

His lips find mine. His pace slows and his kiss deepens. He circles his hips, causing his erection to rub against my G spot once more. The warmth is immediate. I feel so full. A tingle starts deep in my body. It's like it starts at my toes. It's so intense. He notices my reaction and does it again. And again. I'm going to come.

"Come with me, Mia." His voice shakes as he circles his hips again. He doesn't need to tell me twice. I feel his cock swell and that's all I need. My orgasm hits and it's blinding. I grab his arms and hold on. I'm boneless and completed sated. I've never been so satisfied.

As his aftershocks subside, he collapses against me. He's out of breath. It's a scene that I've imagined so many times and it's finally happening. It was so much better than my dreams. He kisses me again, then leans his forehead against mine.

"That was amazing." His smile lights up his whole face. "I want to do this a lot."

I laugh. "Deal."

A knock sounds at the door and I cringe. I'm not ready for this to be over yet. He groans as he pulls out of me. After discarding the condom in the trash, he hands me my dress and waits for me to get dressed before he moves to the door.

"Yo, D Rey." It's Max. He yells through the locked door. "Just wondering if you've seen Mia. I've been looking for her. I'd like to introduce my girlfriend to Oksana."

"Fuck." Damien grabs his shirt off the floor and pulls it over his head.

"Is that code? What's happening?" I straighten my hair in the mirror. Every move I make aches. It's an amazing ache. I know I will feel him every time I move tomorrow.

"I assume Oksana is here and Max is giving me a warning." Damien's hands are fisted at his side and his posture is uneasy.

He opens the door and Max pushes by him. He locks eyes with me and makes a mad dash to my side. He pulls me into an embrace and whispers in my ear. "Make this real, doll. There's media everywhere."

Oksana steps into the room. I want to throw up. She reeks of cheap perfume.   She's   gorgeous   but something's off.   She steps into Damien's space and hugs him. Flashes go off behind her before Mr. Scary, the   bodyguard,   steps   into   the doorframe,   blocking   any   further shots.

"Hi baby." She slurs and kisses his neck. "I've missed you so much." Her eyes burn holes through me.

"What are you doing here?" Damien is cold, his voice strained. Max clears his throat and Damien instantly   goes   into   actor   mode. Another flash goes off and he jumps. "I mean, I didn't expect you to come to the show tonight.   You must be exhausted from all your traveling."

Joshua   moves   the   security guard out of the way and enters the room.   "We have a press conference set up for you. The world is waiting to hear about your engagement." He looks at Max and visibly relaxes. "I've held them off as long as I could. The rest of the guys are already set up. Let's go."

"I'd like to keep our relationship as private as possible." Damien's smile is forced.

"Come on, pookie. We're the biggest story of the year. We can't leave our fans waiting." Oksana pulls his arm.

He looks over his shoulder at me but it's too late. My heart is breaking. Tears fill my eyes. Max takes my hand and smiles down at me. His voice is barely a whisper. "It's ok, Mia. None of this is real. He just needs to play the game. We all do."

"Max, tell us about the woman at your side. Any big announcements from you too?" A journalist scribbles in his notebook as the man next to him snaps our picture. I'm startled by the flashes. I want to run out of here.

Max chuckles next to me. He squeezes my hand in his to give me comfort. "No news from me. She's a special friend. Nothing more. This press conference isn't about me anyway."

I feel like I'm being pulled down by the undertow. The constant noise and flash of the cameras is almost disorienting. All eyes are on me. There's a buzzing around the room. The words mystery woman, relationship with Max Callum and unexpected revelations are thrown around like they're nothing. Max remains calm at my side. Thank God for him. I know he's just trying to help Damien. Maybe this life is too much for me. There are too many secrets already. I feel sick.

"Does this special friend have a name?" Another reporter. I wonder if I could run from the room without being noticed. I suppose the likelihood of that is about the same as a burning meteor crashing to the earth without being seen.

"This is Cathy. She's visiting LA. You don't need to know anything else." He puts his arm around me and I'm instantly relaxed. It's comforting to know he's in this with me. "We'd like to keep things out of the spotlight as much as possible. I know we can count on you to keep us out of the media."

"This question is for Harley. There've been rumors that you've had to up your security detail. Can you confirm that?" The female reporter asks, focusing everyone's attention back on the panel at the front of the room.

I tune out the questions and focus my attention back on Max. "Why are you doing this? I could have just left."

"Mia, you were in his dressing room. The press was all over the place and the minute I saw the wicked witch arrive backstage, I knew I had to do something. No way can you come out of his dressing room without rumors hitting the paper. You have no idea how close we are to losing our contract."

"I'm sorry." I put my head on his chest, enjoying the warmth of his body, the calming beating of his heart. He came to Damien's rescue at the risk of putting himself in the spotlight. Max is the most private of the group, staying out of the tabloids as much as possible. He's quiet at interviews and keeps to himself. I know he's taking a risk for us. He's thrown himself in the line of fire for me and I hardly know him.

"He's only human. Meeting you changed him. It was a good change but he was scared. He's spent half his life running away from anything that matters. He got lost out on the road. Fear is a powerful thing." Max gets quiet, his mind lost in the past. I take the time to study him. His blond hair and boyish good looks make him seem so much younger than he is. "Anyway, we're all a family. If one of us fucks up, we all take the blame. Damien did some shit on the road that wasn't good for our image. We're just all trying to keep shit together so we can get on with the tour."

"Thank you for loving him so much." My voice cracks with emotion. These men are more than a band. They're family and it's beautiful to see. "I don't know how you guys do this. All this attention and micromanaging every second of your lives. I'm glad you have each other."

"Want to get out of here?" Max winks and nods his head toward the exit. "You'll have to trust me."

"Hell yes. Let's go." I giggle when he stands up and offers me his hand. He's so tall and goofy.

As we start to walk toward the exit, the cameras take aim at us. Max throws his arm around my shoulder. "Sorry guys. We don't have much time together. We're gonna go make the best of it."

I make eye contact with Damien. He is holding Oksana's hand, sitting front and center of all the media. His eyes are full of uncertainty. So is my heart. I don't know what to do and I certainly don't know what I'll say to him. Each step away is like ripping my heart out. He only has two more nights in Los Angeles before they hit the road again. There's no going back after what happened tonight. I want him in my life, even if it's just in a small capacity. He's become too important to me. My world doesn't make sense without him. But seeing him as the center of attention, with the woman they call his fiancé wrapped around him, I can't help but think that I don't have the resilience it will take to be a part of this.

Chapter 9

The road has come to an end, it's time for goodbyes. It's ripping me in pieces when you look into my eyes. Life isn't fair, we knew that from the start. I'll keep pieces of you with me, in my dreams, my thoughts, my heart. — Liquid Regret

Joshua is sitting behind his big desk looking all smug. He knows this is ripping me apart. I know he's doing his job. A part of me even knows he's right. But mostly, I'm pissed. How he can think keeping me away from Mia is a good idea blows my mind. I've done everything short of offering to suck his dick. He's not giving in. I feel like a seven year old about to have a temper tantrum. This cannot be happening.

"Damien, let me be clear. You walk through life like nothing can touch you. You didn't give one shit about your image and the image of the band. You had your ass kicked, you fucked everything that moved, and you were threatened with a couple different lawsuits after fighting. You're a liability to the label. When the story hit that you were engaged, they gave you a second look. No one gets a second chance in this industry. No one. You have been granted the impossible."

I scrub my hand down my face. I haven't been able to eat for the past twenty-four hours. Seeing Mia leave with Max made me sick. She called to let me know she was going to take a shift at the aquarium to let her coworker have a day off. Selfishly, I wanted to scream at her that our time was running short. But I couldn't.

She's put up with a lot of shit since I showed back up in her life. With me or not, she heard the stories. I know I meant something to her before I left last year. I hadn't even considered her feelings in all of this.

"For how long? How long do we need to keep this up?" I'm defeated.

"It's not forever. Be seen with Oksana at a couple venues, take her to a couple events. Paste on a smile and let the world believe you love her. If things get too hard and Mia decides she wants to come see a few shows, we fly her in. Max can pick her up at the airport. He's agreed to be seen with her when needed."

"He's agreed to be seen with her." I scratch my head. Like it's so fucking difficult to be seen with her. "So we all live this big lie and everyone stays miserable."

"Everyone stays employed." Joshua stands up and shakes my hand. "Go do whatever it is you want to do before we head back out. The tour isn't forever. I know it might feel like that but it won't be long until you're back here and you can live your life the way you want to."

"You're doing the right thing, bro." Harley slaps me on the shoulder. Always the voice of reason. "Be honest with Mia. Tell her how you feel. Give her a reason to fight for the relationship. It's not going to be easy but it won't be forever. She's worth it, man."

"Ok." I can't think of anything else to say. It's all been said. I laid my cards out on the table for the band. It's time to do the same thing for Mia. I'll fight for her until the day I die.

The drive to the aquarium isn't long. I loved coming here as a kid. Walking through the lobby brings back so many memories. I miss how carefree my life was then. I miss how loving and safe things were. I miss running through the halls with Steve, racing each other to the shark tank to get the best seat to watch them swim. I miss his laugh as my mom would yell at me to slow down.

"Damien?" Her voice pulls me from my past. "What are you doing here?"

She's keeping her distance. It's been twenty minutes and I've already forgotten I can't be seen with her in public. "Is there somewhere we can talk?"

She shrugs. "Sure. I'm heading into the theater to rehearse with a very unwilling dolphin. You could come with me if you'd like."

"Unwilling, huh?" I follow her. "What is it that you've asked him to do? Maybe it's beneath him. Maybe he's shy?"

She laughs. "We lost one of our dolphins last week. He'd been taken out of the shows a couple months ago. He was old and it wasn't unexpected." She bends over and taps the surface. I jump back as a head breaks free of the water. "Don't be such a girl."

She zips up her wetsuit and jumps into the water. When she breaks the surface, so does the dolphin. I'm witnessing something that could bring tears to my eyes. She blows her whistle and the creature spins in a circle before splashing her in the face. She laughs, the love apparent in her eyes.

"Want to swim with us?" Mia calls out to me. Hell yes I do. "Grab one of the suits over on the hooks and come on in."

I pull the suit on and watch in awe as she communicates with the bottlenose. She blows a series of whistles, each one commanding a different trick. She feeds him tiny fish when he gets something right. Seeing her like this, in her element, doing what she loves, makes me realize I could never ask her to give it up and join me on the road. We can make this work. We don't need to figure it all out right now.

"Stormy, this is my friend Damien. Can you give him a kiss?" She motions to him and he kisses me on the mouth. "He looks like he didn't like that. What do we think of that?" Another hand motion and Stormy blows air at me and it sounds ridiculously close to taunting.

"Why would you want to kiss me when she's right here? She's gorgeous. Certainly you see that." I rub my hand across his face. He's soft like satin. "This is incredible, Mia." I don't think I've smiled this much in weeks.

"Want to try something even better?" She smiles at me and all I can do is nod. "Swim over to the side. Stop about six feet from the edge. Do not panic."

She's laughing so I'm instantly scared. "Why? What are you doing?"

"Trust me." She motions to Stormy and blows the whistle. He goes under water and I can't see him. "When you feel him, push your legs down and try to stand. Just go with it."

My heart is pounding. I feel him under me. I lock my legs and push up. I'm being pushed through the water. Just before we reach the other edge of the pool, he lets me go. It's an adrenaline rush like no other. Mia is clapping and giving Stormy a fish.

"Congratulations,   Mr. Reynolds. You mastered the foot push on the first try." She swims towards me, her face completely void of makeup, her hair soaked. I could search the entire world and never find anyone more beautiful. "What'd you think?"

"I think you have the best job in the world." I reach for her without thinking. I need her. My lips meet hers, my tongue begging for entry. She sighs and melts into me. I claim her mouth and I tell her everything I can't say with words.

Water splashes us and Mia pulls away laughing. She splashes Stormy back. He clicks and whistles, happy to be in the same place she is. I don't blame him. She raises her hands and he rockets from the water, propelling himself upright and through the water with the strength of his back fin. When he dives below the water, she blows her whistle. He comes up under her, launching her into the air before she dives back into the water. I have never been envious of anyone. But in this moment, I envy the life she has. Her joy is written all over her face. This breathtaking mammal put her smile there. I'm not embarrassed to admit, I'm jealous of a dolphin.

"Thank you for this." She smiles as she swims to me. "He's always showing off when someone else is here with us." He needed this. He's been so down since his buddy died. He relies on me to feed him and love him. He has no idea that I rely on him to love me back. He's amazing therapy."

"He's not the only one." Shit. The words are out before I even know what I've said. She stops swimming and stares at me. I need to touch her. I pull her to me, it's now or never. "Do you have any idea how I feel?"

She bites her lip, tears forming in her eyes. She doesn't speak. Just shakes her head and looks into my eyes. I can feel her shaking.

"I don't know what this is. But I want to find out. I've never felt this way. It scares the shit out of me." I pull her into a tight hug. "You've stayed with me, Mia. No matter where I went, part of you was there with me."

"I feel the same way." She wraps her legs around me. "I just don't know if I'm strong enough to deal with everything you have to deal with."

"Baby, let me deal with all the hard stuff. I just want you to be here when I get home. Will you be?"

"Not if things are the same way they were the last time you went out on the road." She's being honest. I hurt her. I won't do it again.

"You mean more to me than that. I hope you'll trust me long enough to prove it to you."

She smiles. "You leave tomorrow?" I nod my head. "Then come home with me tonight and show me why you're worth waiting for."

"That sounds a lot like a dare, Ms. Lee." I laugh when she splashes me. "I plan on making sure you can't forget me even if you try."

Chapter 10

My heart is pounding while I wait for Damien. I've made him lasagna, salad, and crunchy garlic bread. My mouth is watering. My apartment smells amazing. I can't wait to dig in, fill my belly and then spend the rest of the night lost in him.

He leaves tomorrow. It's like déjà vu. I know that my heart will feel shattered in the morning. Watching him walk away the first time was hard. The second time will be impossible. But this time, there's hope. He'll be coming home eventually. And he knows exactly where I am.

A knock. Here go the butterflies. My hands are sweating.

Why? I shake my head trying to focus. I reach for the knob, take a deep breath and open up my heart to all that he has to offer.

"Hi honey. I'm home." He kicks the door shut with his foot. "Come here."

I lean into him and he attacks my mouth. He takes hold of my cheeks, holding me captive against his mouth. Heat pools between my thighs. I can feel his excitement growing against my belly. The dinner might've been a waste. I need him.

He spins me around, pinning me against the door. His hands are frantic, unbuttoning my shorts and shoving them to the ground. He leans into me and pulls a condom from his pocket. His pants fall around his ankles. He rolls the condom on like a pro. Before I can even form a coherent thought, he pushes into me. "Dinner smells amazing." He leans in and sniffs my neck. "But you smell even better."

When he begins to move, I lock my ankles behind his back. My body is on fire. The door shakes on its hinges as he pumps into me. He bites my neck, then soothes it with kisses. His tongue traces my neck, my jaw. I feel him breathing in my ear and I shiver.

He fills me completely. My body was made for him. He pulls almost all the way out and pushes back in. It feels unbelievable. Just when I think it can't get better, he pulls all the way out and circles my clit with the head of his penis.

"Oh my god."

"You like that?" He does it again and I start to tremble. "Oh yeah.

You do like that. I'll take you right to the edge but I want you to come on my cock."

His voice is my undoing. My orgasm is building. My body is on high alert. I'm going to explode. He pulls his cock away, leaving me begging for more. "Please, Damien. I'm so close."

He circles my clit one last time and slides back in just as I come apart. My orgasm makes me scream. My walls tighten, milking him. He moans and bites my shoulder. His legs shake. He's fighting hard not to come. He takes a deep breath and starts to move again.

His pace is more frantic. "Your pussy feels so good. So wet. I want to feel your come dripping down my legs like it did backstage." He presses his thumb to my clit, his dick pounding into me. "I want to hear you scream."

It's too much. I'm like a live wire. The electricity between us sparks. My pupils are blown with pleasure. His breathing is erratic, his eyes almost closed in ecstasy. I come so hard, I may pass out. I throw myself against him as my legs loosen from his waist. I'm completely at his mercy.

"That's my girl. Do you feel that?" He grunts as he continues his assault. "I was made to fuck you. Only you, Mia."

I can feel my pleasure pour from my body. No one has ever made me feel so good, so alive, so on fire. I shove against him, pushing away from the door. He momentarily loses his balance as I drop to the floor and pull him back into me. I rip the condom from him and take him into my mouth. He's already so close but I need to taste him. I need him to lose his mind.

I need him to feel a fraction of what he makes me feel.

"Holy fuck." He braces his hands on the door behind me. I take him all the way into my mouth, humming as he hits the back of my throat.

I hold onto his perfect ass as he fucks my mouth. My other hand finds that sensitive spot just under his balls and his legs almost give out. I press and feel his dick swell. His whole body convulses as he empties himself into my mouth.

He roars as he comes. "Fuck, Mia." It's the hottest thing I have ever heard. I did this to him and I'm proud of myself. I smile as I lick him clean.

He drops to his knees and pulls me to his mouth. His kiss is possessive. He already owns me. He owns every part of me. He moans when my tongue enters his mouth. The sound is heaven. I'm ready for round two. Just like the last time we said goodbye, we won't be getting any sleep. Only this time is different. This time, I plan on spending every second making him understand how much he truly means to me.

The morning sun is my enemy. My stomach rolls at the thought of Damien leaving. He opened up to me last night and told me everything. He was emotional and broken as he explained the need to keep up appearances with Oksana. He praised Max for subjecting himself to the lie. He warned me about paparazzi and what life might be like. I didn't care about any of it. I'm so completely in love that I will do whatever it takes to be a part of him. I know he feels the same way. He didn't say the words I long to hear. But everything he did say, every emotion he let me see, confirmed what I think I've known all along. Our week last year meant just as much to him as it did to me.

"I never thought I could feel so high and so low at the same time." He stretches his arms above his head. His body is perfection. His arms are covered in tattoos, his chest and abs covered in muscle. His dark hair is tangled and standing up in every direction after spending the night having the hottest sex of our lives.

"I can feel the darkness creeping into my heart." I giggle and cry at the same time.

"Don't cry. We're in Seattle at Rock Fest next weekend. We'll get you there. I'll get my own room. We'll make this work."

"Won't Oksana be there?" I can't help the tears. I'm such a girl.

"I'll talk to her. She'll understand as long as I promise to keep the lie alive. She's crazy but she's not heartless." He rubs my back as I lay my head on his chest. It's going to be the longest week of my life.

"Thank you." I rub my hand over his abs. He shivers.

"For what?" He kisses the top of my head. Falling in love with him was so natural. It was as easy as breathing.

"For calming me down in the elevator. For making me see we were worth the risk. For picking me."

"Baby, I would pick you every single time."

As the alarm goes off on his phone, we hold each other. My heart is in my throat. His hold is tight and I don't complain. I don't want him to ever let go. Walking him to the door makes my heart shatter.

"You're everything to me, Mia." He leans his forehead against mine. It's all the contact we need. His eyes tell me everything. He loves me too.

I watch through the bedroom window as he drives away. The apartment is suddenly completely silent. I can't breathe. I curl into a ball on my bed. I'm exhausted, emotionally and physically. It's only a week and I made it a whole year before now. Of course, my heart feels so much more invested than it had before. My feelings are stronger. Sex changes everything. I knew that when I went backstage with exactly that in mind.

I'm in and out of sleep. My cell phone is on my nightstand but it's silent. My tearstained cheeks burn, my eyes are on fire. I know I need to drag myself out of my bed, take a shower and get ready for tomorrow's shift at work. Life goes on. I need to remind myself that I survive every day because I choose to and it's ok to be sad. If I choose to be in his life, I need to get used to being away from him. Maybe I need to get in touch with Harley's wife for some advice on how to survive. As the tears start again, I turn onto my stomach and bury my face in my pillow.

The bed dips and I jump. Steve puts his hand on my back and smiles. "Hey."

I sit up and lean into him, letting go of every shred of sorrow. He holds me, rubs my back and rocks back and forth. Thank God he found my sister. Thank God he's going to be my brother. He's more than I could've asked for. I have no idea how long he's held me. It could be five minutes, it could be an hour. I have no concept of time when I'm this emotional and exhausted.

"Why are you here?" My voice is hoarse.

"D called on his way out of town. Thought you might need some company." His wink tells me he knows everything.

"Thank you." I smile as he wipes the last of the tears from my cheeks.

"I wouldn't be anywhere else tonight. You're almost my sister. He's blood.   Family first. Besides, he sounded so pathetic I couldn't say no." Steve pulls me from the bed and pushes me toward the bathroom. "Get in the shower, you stink. I brought pizza. We'll watch some terrible reality TV. Hurry."

I laugh. "Fine. Anything but that dance shit you and Lily watch."

"Blasphemy, woman.   That show is sacred." He laughs from the kitchen.

I smile at myself in the mirror. As brother in laws go, I hit the jackpot. I think I'll keep him.

Chapter 11

Losing memory and hope every night,
until I hold you again, life isn't right.
I'm lost, It's dark, I'm bleeding, I'm cold. I
need your touch, I need your soul.
– Liquid Regret

"Griff, heads up." I throw Harley my notebook. I've spent the last three hours with my head buried in the pages, attempting to create our next masterpiece. The tour bus is like a second home but today it's hard to get comfortable. The drive to Salt Lake City will take hours. I need the distraction. Anything to take my mind off of Mia. I can't help but wonder what she's doing. I hope Steve is with her. He's probably making her watch that piece of shit show that he and Lily are obsessed with. I chuckle when I picture Mia sitting through that.

Harley holds the notebook in his hands and continues to stare out the window. It's always hard for him to leave Della but this time seems different. I make my way to where he's sitting and sit across from him. He makes eye contact but doesn't speak.

"What's up?"

"Sorry, man." He flips open the notebook but I reach forward and stop him.

"Griff, what's wrong?" Years of friendship and I can read him like a book. "He's scared."

He leans forward and speaks in a hushed voice. "Del got a threatening letter. It was left at her office. I called her boss and resigned for her. I can't handle this shit. I feel helpless."

"Nobody saw who left it?" I will personally kill anyone that harms one hair on her head. She's my family and no one fucks with my family.

"The receptionist said she was blond and skinny. Said she was nervous and kept looking around. She asked a couple times if Della was there. I don't know, man. I want her to come on the road with us. I don't like her alone in the house."

"Why the fuck isn't she on the bus?" I'm pissed.

"She's gone to Santa Barbara with a couple friends. I tried to get her to cancel but you know Del. She's hardheaded and independent. She said she isn't going to let some crazy bitch control her life. I've got tracking devices on everything. I hired an extra guard. I don't know what else I can do." Harley rubs his hands on his jeans.

"She'll be ok. We'll get her on the bus in Seattle. She can't say no if we tie her up and bring her against her will." I laugh when Harley shakes his head. "Steve and Lil have a ton of room. She could stay there awhile. Until all this blows over."

"Thanks, man. Enough about the crazy shit. How's Mia?"

I grin like a big pussy. I'm whipped. "She's the one. If I wasn't engaged to Oksana, I'd marry her today."

Harley laughs and I can't help but join him. This whole thing is a clusterfuck, caused by my superb coping skills. Tomorrow I will talk to

Oksana, today I act like it isn't happening.

"How about her crazy friend? Laney is it? She seems cool. Have to keep Chance away from her. She's exactly the type he fucks over." He kicks the seat in front of him.

"Fuck you, Harley." Chance laughs. "I'm too pretty for her. She says I'm not her type. She likes the pierced nipples and tattoos."

Max lowers his sunglasses at the mention of nipples. This dysfunctional group is my family. I couldn't be more proud.

Harley will be there to pick you up tomorrow. Don't let Laney lick him. See you then, beautiful!

I've been waiting all week to send that text. I wish it could be me picking them up. But, as the face of the band, my entire day is scheduled with radio interviews and appearances. It's probably good that Griffin goes anyway. He's spent the entire week stressing out about his wife.

Counting the seconds.

Even her text messages put a smile on my face. We've been to four cities in the last five days. Two of the groupies wore the same perfume that she does. I was instantly hard. Nothing like meeting fans when my dick is throbbing in my pants. She has taken up residence in my brain. When I do sleep, I have the best dreams.

The shows have been flawless. We're at the top of our game. The stadiums are sold out and record sales are off the charts. Joshua has been with us all week. We chose him as our manager because of how hands on he is. Even when he's busting my balls, I wouldn't trade him for anyone else in the world. The label has ceased all talks of canning me. Guess the engagement story is working. Unfortunately, that means we have to keep it up for a while.

Della and Oksana will be on the plane. Don't freak. She's fine with it.

I hold my breath waiting for her response. Mia's cool. I assume the news won't even shake her. Oksana and I have an agreement. As long as I keep my relationship with Mia behind closed doors, she won't make a scene. Besides, she seems much more interested in Harley and Chance than she is me anyway. She's crazier than shit. But if she stays quiet, I'm fine. Maybe I can slip some Prozac into some cheese. It works for dogs.

K. As long as we have time together.

She doesn't get it. I lust her. I would give up this world for her. There isn't anyone that will keep us apart. I will blow this entire rouse before I lose this girl. Honestly, I think it will be good for Oksana to meet Mia. Maybe it will help if she sees that this story isn't good for me. If we're unified, I can't imagine that we won't be able to say there was a breakup and we remain civil. This story brought her tons of attention. She's gotten work again, despite her obvious addiction. Shit. Did I act like that? If I did, I was an asshole.

I should turn in early tonight but I know it'll be hard to sleep knowing that tomorrow, I'll be wrapped around Mia. We have a two hour drive by tour bus early in the morning. The music fest is a huge outdoor concert with ten different bands and two different stages. We were nobodies last year. This year, we headline. What a difference a year makes. I can't help but smile. We worked hard and we made it. I pray that tomorrow is the one day of sunshine that Seattle gets during the year.

The ringing of the phone scares me. It's Harley. "What's up man?"

"I'm flying out at 7. Make sure Max is at the hotel at 10. I'll drop Mia and Laney off to him."

"Thanks for doing this, bro."

"Just be pretty for those cameras." Griffin loves to make fun of me. He knows I hate doing the appearances. "Our image depends on it."

"Do me a favor? Don't let Oksana close to Mia."

Harley laughs and hangs up the phone. Wonder if it's too late to cancel all the appearances tomorrow?

Chapter 12

She's weird. There's no other word to describe her. I pictured this larger than life, gorgeous, can't take your eyes off her, model. She's not any of that. She's pretty. No question about that. But she's way too skinny. Her eyes are rimmed with dark circles. Her blond hair is a mess. I'm trying to be discrete but I'm sure she knows I'm sizing her up. She did the same thing to me when I walked onto the plane.

While Harley talks to the pilot, I decide to kick back and enjoy. I've never been on a private jet. Heck, I've never really been anywhere. It smells like leather and fresh brewed coffee. My mouth waters. The white seats are comfortable and lie back so far, I feel like I'm in bed. Laney and I are facing Della and what I assume is Harley's seat. The stewardess gave me a warm cloth when I got on the plane. It's a little taste of heaven. I'm waiting to wake up from the dream I'm having.

Della's head is buried in her book but she smiles at me when she sees me looking at her. She's the beautiful one. Her olive complexion, her silky hair, her bright eyes. It's what I would picture a model looking like. She winks at me and laughs. "I'm glad you're coming with us."

"I'm sorry. I don't mean to stare. I'm a little nervous about all this." I sweep my hand in the air, tilting my head in Oksana's direction. "I feel like the other woman."

Della closes her book and leans forward. "Honestly babe, she won't even remember you were on the plane. She's totally strung out." Her voice is barely a whisper. "She calls me Diane. I've known her for a few years. She either hates me or she's that clueless. I'd bet on the latter."

I frown. It's sad. She's throwing her life away. I've never been addicted to anything so I'm not the expert on it. I just can't imagine someone with that much potential throwing it all way. She throws a fake smile my way. My return smile is genuine. I want to like her. It would make life easier. I just wish we weren't all blanketed with this lie.

"Can I get you anything, Mia?" Harley's voice startles me back. I shake my head no. Looking around this plane, I can't imagine anything else I'd ever need.

"How about you?" It's like I can see that lust rolling off Laney as she looks at Harley.

"Wine?" She's using her sultry voice.

"I'll get it." Della jumps up, pointing to the seat so Harley will sit down.

Laney rolls her eyes. "Making your wife get it?"

Harley pulls something from his pocket and holds it up. "It's my one year chip. It took me four years to get it. I've been sober two years next weekend."

My eyes widen. Laney shifts in her seat. Kill me now. Harley just laughs and rolls it between his fingers.

His smile meets his eyes. He's breathtaking.

"It's fine. Stop panicking. You can drink in front of me. Every single day is a struggle. But, it's mine and I own it." He puts the chip back in his pocket and takes a bottle of water from Della's hands. "Thank you, gorgeous."

I want to melt. Their love is so beautiful. He takes her hand and kisses her knuckles. Her head rests on his shoulder as we take off. There's no one else in the world for either of them. That's what I want. The kind of love that people would die for. The kind of love that everyone can see.

I lean back and try to relax. I've been on edge for a week. I can't wait to see Damien. He's occupied every second of my life since he crashed back into it. I have told my heart not to rush it. Damn thing has a mind of its own. My brain is a little smarter, but not by much. This weekend will give me a good glimpse of how things will be. It will also be a test of how strong I am. Seeing Damien with Oksana will be tough. I don't think I'm a very jealous person. Still, I've never been in a situation like this. It's completely screwed up.

What happened to the whole fairytale? What happened to the prince riding up on the horse and rescuing me from the tower? I imagined things so differently. I was convinced that Damien would find me someday. I'd hoped he would drop everything and pursue me until I was his. Instead, he ran into me by accident at a bar. A bar where the former drug addict took his recovering alcoholic friend. It made no sense that they were there. He'd pursued me but only because the elevator had broken down and trapped us inside. Holy shit. I can't help but giggle.

"Are you overthinking again?" Laney looks over and starts to laugh. She never knows what we're laughing at but once she laughs, I laugh even harder.

"I was just feeling sorry for myself because I didn't get the whole white horse, riding off into the sunset thing. But they were in a bar. The two people who should never, ever go into a bar. And it was the one we were in. What are the odds? And then my elevator trapped us inside. What are the odds of that?" My laughter continues. It's a nervous habit that I do every time I overthink anything.

"Stop overthinking, Mimi. For once in your life, just take a chance. Not all fairytales have horses and sunsets. Some of them start in bars and end in elevators." What would I do without her? Then she burps and reminds me I can't take her anywhere.

Harley shakes his head and gets up. "Sexy, Lane. Real sexy."

Della giggles. "Laney's laugh is contagious. It's kind of a cackle."

Laney's jaw drops and she huffs before she belly laughs again. Her laugh is exactly like a cackle. It's not at all feminine and it's loud. When we're in public, everyone looks at us. She loves the attention. She can have it. I don't want it. But I wouldn't trade that part of her for anything.

Harley has moved and is sitting across from Oksana. She's in tears and I can't help but notice how affectionate he is with her. I'm stumped for a minute. Naturally, I stare. Can you blame me? She is definitely coming down from a high. She's sweaty and nervous. He wipes her tears and holds her hands. His whispered voice is hard to make out but hers isn't.

"Why can't I have you?" She pouts.

He just smiles, his voice a little louder. "Because of her." He points at Della and smiles.

"I'm sorry. I would kick her ass right now if I were you. That's fucking ballsy. Why are you just sitting there?" Laney glares at Harley but directs her question at Della.

"Griffin's the mother hen of the group. He's not happy unless everyone's happy. He's made it his mission to try to save her. I think he sees so much of himself in her addiction." She calmly looks at her husband and then back at us. "I've never doubted his feelings for me. Not even for a second. We've been together so long, I don't know where he stops and I start. He'd never do anything to hurt me. She's harmless. And if he can save her, then what an amazing gift that would be."

My eyes fill with tears. Is this woman human? Everything about her is soft. Her skin, her voice, her heart. She's got best friend potential. If I get to be with Damien, and this is the life we live, then I'll be so happy to have her by my side.

"Shit. I see why he loves you. If you weren't married, I'd propose right now." Laney holds her glass up and clinks Della's water bottle. "And you're hot."

"You're all hot." Harley sits down and puts his arm around his wife. "I say the four of us go check out the bedroom in the back."

He laughs as Della punches him in the arm. "In your dreams, buddy boy."

"Yeah. Mia here is too hung up on your fearless leader. And you couldn't handle this. I'd tie you up and make you call me Mommy. You wouldn't last a minute."

"Laney." My face is bright red and I'm looking around for the emergency exit. I may push her out. She just laughs at me and winks at Della. No fear.

Harley leans into her and whispers in her ear. "I'm faster and I'm stronger and I submit to no one. I'd ruin you, babe. And that just wouldn't be fair to all the men you plan on torturing in the future."

It's possible Adelaine Jones just met her match. This trip is going to be interesting. Della just shakes her head and looks back down at her book. I want to be her when I grow up. She's the strongest woman I've ever met.

A sense of dread comes over me as I lean back to close my eyes. I don't know what it is but I can't seem to shake it. I take a deep breath. Something isn't right. I look around but everything seems perfectly abnormal. Exactly as it had been. Laney is laughing, Harley is giving her hell, Della is smiling and even Oksana seems to be settling into the trip. I need to stop with all the Criminal Minds marathons. My imagination is working overtime.

I'm not sure I'll ever get used to this. The flash bulbs are blinding. I can see Max coming toward us and I smile. He's so tall and handsome. I'm not sure what he has to gain from stepping into this story but I'm relieved he has. There's something calming about him. He makes me feel safe. He towers over me and there's comfort in that.

"Sorry about all this. They followed the tour bus in. Doesn't matter which entrance we use. They're everywhere." Max hugs me and tucks my hair behind my ear. "How are you, Red?"

"I'm better now." I giggle when he puts his arm around me. The cameras go crazy. "This is insane. Do you ever get used to it?"

"Sadly, they start to fade into the background. As long as they aren't chasing you in a car or stepping right into your personal space, you learn to ignore them." He picks up my suitcase and takes my hand. "Let's head up and you guys can get settled."

Laney raises her eyebrows as she takes in the beauty that is Max Callum. Hiding behind his drum set, he's out of the spotlight. It's a shame. He's gorgeous. He's got the old Hollywood movie star look. His jaw is square, his face chiseled. His blond hair is perfectly disheveled. You could get lost in his gray blue eyes. And his personality is just as beautiful. I wish Laney would settle down with someone like him. I know it's a long shot. He's clean cut and free of tattoos. Not at all her type but I can still dream.

When the elevator doors finally shut, I take a deep breath. "Thank you, Max." I hug him.

"Anytime, Red. I needed a little more excitement in my life." Max laughs and I know that no matter what ever happens, he will always be someone I call a friend. "We'll head over to the show in a few hours. Settle in. Order some room service. Whatever you guys want. I'm right next door, so if you need anything, just knock."

Chapter 13

You'll call me sir as you shatter on cue
A flick of my tongue, I'll own you. –
Liquid Regret

The crowd is massive. The fairgrounds are packed, bodies bumping, heat blazing. Both stages are in full swing. Bands are everywhere. It's almost like a dream. Last year, this was us. The small acts were early in the day. The crowds are larger this year. The energy is buzzing. I'm having a hard time containing my excitement.

Part of it is that I'll see Mia in just a few minutes. Max sent me a text when they left the hotel. My body is already on fire. I've missed her this week. Oksana arrived about an hour ago. We did the obligatory photos for the press, held hands, smiled. It's all bullshit. Since I told her about Mia, she's been distant. I'm not sure what it means but it makes it easier when she isn't all over me. Thank God for small favors.

I always know the second the rest of the band arrives. There's a shift in energy. The crowd screams and the photographers circle them like prey. The only privacy I've seen here is behind the B stage. It backs up into the woods and the last act there tonight is a local band that's in the middle of a big scandal. It should be pretty quiet and may be my only chance to get Mia alone tonight.

"Max." The flashbulbs are popping. Since he and Mia became 'an item', he's had a ton of attention.

He's a superhero for doing this for me. He hates the spotlight.

Della and Harley join me as I stare Mia down. Della wraps her arms around me like she always does. Aside from Harley, she's the closest person in the world to me. I would protect her with my life. With all the shit going on with Harley, I feel an overwhelming responsibility to protect her. She saved my life once. It's time to return the favor.

As soon as Mia joins us, my heart starts to hammer behind my ribs. She smells amazing. Her green eyes are bright and happy. The pull to her is overwhelming. I want to hug her. I want to kiss her. Shit, I want to do a hell of a lot more than that. I step forward and hug Laney first. I need to make this look friendly and obvious. When I pull away, I fist bump

Max. The vultures are circling. Mia tenses when I hug her. I'm trying. I really am. But it's hard to act like her friend.

"You look gorgeous," I whisper in her ear and she shivers. She's mine. Hands down.

Max clears his throat and puts his arm around her. She smiles up at him. Part of me wants to kick his ass. I want to punch that smug smile off his face. She seems comfortable with him. I need to pull my head out of my ass. Green is not my color.

"You're up in two hours. Sound check in one. Head on over to stage A and get situated backstage. They've got tents set up so find a seat and stay put." Josh is barking commands, trying to herd us away from the cameras. We value our time before a show and the sooner we get out of the spotlight, the more we'll all relax.

The word backstage is seriously a joke here. They have four white tents set up. Makeup and hair is set up in two and the other two have places to relax and stuff our faces with all kinds of shit that will slow me down on stage. The things artists ask for always make me laugh. I'm happy with a bottle of water and some fruit. Afterwards, I'll stuff my face with pizza and fast food. Before, I need quiet and I need to hydrate.

I've spent the last ten minutes kicked back in a lounge chair with the makeshift air conditioner blowing at my feet. The sound check was quicker than I thought it would be. Sitting here, I have the perfect view of Mia and Laney, relaxing with glasses of champagne. Della joined them about five minutes ago and is telling them stories about the band. Hearing Mia's laugh calms my nerves. I want to fast forward through the show and get her back to the hotel. I need to find a way to keep my brain and my heart on the same page. My brain knows what has to be done. My heart has a mind of its own and it's completely out of control.

"It's time." Chance smiles down at me as he throws the guitar strap over his shoulder.

One more deep breath and I'm ready. I wink at Mia and follow Chance around to the side of the stage. Security is all around Harley as we line up to start the show. I miss the days of having a few minutes alone with the guys before we're on.

"Ladies and Gentleman, Liquid Regret." Joshua's voice echoes as the screams start. I hear Max pounding on his drums, dry ice lifts from the stage, it's eerie and I love it. Griffin and Chance run on stage as the lights change. I shut my eyes and I'm in the zone. The only thing that exists is my music. The only thing I know is lyrics. It's all I am.

The guitars scream into the night. The wind picks up. I take the steps two at a time and take center stage. My voice is rough from being outside. It's exactly the sound that the crowd responds to. It happens by accident but it is the best sound we get. I can see Mia in the front row, dancing with Della, Oksana and Laney. It's like a dream, having the woman I'm crazy for enjoying my music just feet away from me.

"We've got a little something we've been working on." The end of my sentence is drowned out by screams. "We're gonna try it out for you tonight. You ready to get dirty?"

I can't help but chuckle. I never knew what the word swoon actually meant. Now, I know and I can't believe that people do it over me and the rest of these bastards that are up on this stage.

On your knees, your mouth is home
Your body, your mind, your soul I own
you moan, you soar, you writhe, you   scream
This is real. A hot, wet dream.

You'll call me sir as you shatter on cue
A flick of my tongue, I'll own you

We wrote the lyrics on the tour bus two nights ago. It was effortless and fell together easier than anything we've ever written. Our usual lyrics are dark, cold. This song, shit. It's

Mia. I want to own her. I want to own every single inch of her.

Our set is over before I know it. The crowd is spent, sweating, turned on. It's exactly how I like to leave them. The lights go dark, security is on stage rushing us off. There are no encores tonight. I need to get to Mia. My body is on fire and she's the only thing to put out the flames.

I see Joshua out of the corner of my eye. He's pushing Oksana, Laney and Mia toward our holding area backstage. There aren't any press conferences scheduled tonight. It's a small miracle and I couldn't be more thankful. Oksana is at my side before I know it. She's waving to the crowd that has gathered outside the tent. Max is ahead of us, pulling Mia by the hand. She's flushed and smiling and I want to scream. My heart is so torn.

It's like I'm having to choose the band or Mia. I don't know why I can't have both.

"Come with me." Harley grabs me and Oksana and heads out the side of the tent at a run. Max and Mia are right behind us. They want to get us out of the spotlight as quickly as possible.

Something has changed. Joshua stays behind with security, holding the cameras at bay. Della is being pushed onto the tour bus by the head of security. Chance is pushing Laney through the door as he yells at the few people that have gathered around the bus. Oksana trips, sending the three of us head first into the pavement. Harley's hands are quick, grabbing her before impact. I'm not so lucky. I feel the concrete rip my jeans, my arm scrapes against the rocks. The sting is instant but welcoming. I am usually so numb after a show and this snaps life back into focus.

"Go." I wave Harley off as he throws Oksana over his shoulder and sprints the rest of the way to the bus. Getting him to Della is more important than having him help me up. Max and Mia stop. She kneels next to me and brushes the loose pavement off my arm. Her eyes are concerned as she takes in the scrape. It hits me like a ton of bricks. I'm in love with her. Not just questioning if this is love. Not just wondering if this is what it should feel like. Not just worrying about getting it wrong. I can't fucking breathe. I grab at my t-shirt, trying to catch my breath. I'm being suffocated. I rip it over my head, gulping for air. "Holy shit."

"What hurts?" She puts her hands on my shoulders. "Are you ok?"

"I love you."

Her eyes are wide. She looks around and locks eyes with Max. He's pinching the bridge of his nose and shaking his head. When she looks back at me, her eyes are filled with tears. "What?" Her voice is a whisper.

Max pulls me to my feet and points between the busses. "Through there. Go. My driver is waiting. I'll go with the bus. No one can see you. Do you understand me?"

I don't have to be told twice. I pull Mia through the line of buses into the edge of the woods. It's dark and quiet. The black Town Car is waiting and I realize I'm almost at a full sprint when Mia starts laughing. She's windblown, flushed, out of breath. I need her. I can't wait any longer.

I practically dive into the back seat, pulling her into my lap so she's straddling me. Her hair spills around us. My lips are on her neck, her jaw, her ear. I'm frantic. "Fuck me, Mia."

"The driver." Her fear is instantly forgotten when I run my fingers into her dress and find her core. She tenses and her eyes widen but slam shut when I dip into her. She moans and lets her head fall back. Her hips roll against my hand. She's ready and I can't wait another second.

"Give me your cell phone." I yell up to the driver. He throws it over the seat to me. He's about to get a show and it isn't one I want recorded. The car starts to roll forward. We have about ten minutes.

Mia's hands fumble with my jeans. I pull a condom out of my back pocket and hand it to her before pulling my jeans down to my knees. I'm sheathed and ready. When she slides down me, my eyes cross. This is home.

Chapter 14

I don't know what's happening to me. I've always been a private person. I just can't help myself around Damien. I'd probably crawl on stage and drop my clothes if he asked me to. Last time, it was a dressing room. Hearing Chance having sex was such a turn on. Now I'm in the back seat of a car, a stranger driving us back to a hotel. I don't care. If I don't get Damien inside of me, I feel like I won't survive.

He hands me a condom and I rip it open with my teeth. After I roll it on, I slide down his shaft. I'm soaked. I circle my hips and his eyes close. I grip his shoulders and pull myself against him harder. Fuck, this feels good.

Every part of his body fits perfectly against mine.

I need him deeper. I arch my back, gripping his knees with my hands. I ride him hard, every part of my body consumed by pleasure. His cock rubs against my G-spot, over and over and over. I'm chanting something incoherent. I can hear the driver's breathing change. I know he's turned on and that just intensifies this for me. Electricity shoots up my legs, coils in my belly and I explode, my body crumbling against Damien as wave after wave of pleasure grips his cock, milking him, begging him for release.

Damien grabs my hips, driving his shaft into me as far as he can go. Sweat beads on his forehead. His hips piston, his cock drives into me faster and faster. My body clenches around him. "This pussy is mine. You can walk around with Max at your side and be all smiles. But this is mine. Tell me, Mia. Who owns you?"

He pinches my clit and I scream. "You do." I can't breathe. The pleasure is too much. My toes curl and my body tightens. I watch him as he pulls his fingers from between us and sucks them into his mouth. His eyes close as he moans. My orgasm is just out of reach. He knows it and he's taunting me.

"You want to come, Mia?" He smirks and I want to cry. The pleasure is building and I can't control my body. "Get ready."

He licks his finger, reaches around behind me and inserts it into my ass. The sensation is too much. I shatter into pieces, screaming, riding his finger and his cock. The orgasm is fierce, the strongest I have ever had. I can't hear anything, I can't open my eyes. All I can do is feel.

Damien growls low in his throat. It's so sexy and sends me into another orgasm. My body is on fire. I collapse against him and feel him swell before emptying himself into the condom. We're both soaked, panting, sated.

His grip loosens from my hips and he pulls me into a hug. "I fucking love you, Mia." He bites my shoulder then licks away the sting.

"I love you, too," I whisper against his chest as we pull up in back of the hotel. The sudden truth of what we've done in front of the driver hits me. I blush and bury my head against his shoulder. "I can't believe we just did that."

"My Mia is a little bit of an exhibitionist." He rolls me off of him and toward the door. "It's sexy as hell."

He reaches across me and opens the door. Max is standing against the back wall with his arms crossed. He smirks when he catches my eye. Busted. I go from being completely fearless to giggling with nerves. I feel like I've just been caught doing something I shouldn't. When he sees my blush, he laughs and helps pull me from the car.

Damien stays behind, talking to the driver. I'm so glad I'm not part of that conversation. I duck under Max's arm, feeling safe. He chuckles and shakes his head. He'd lay his life down for Damien. It makes him honorable. It also makes him amazing and I know that I will spend forever making sure he knows I would do the same for him. "Laney is down with Della and Griff."

I laugh as I fumble with my keycard. "I feel a little dirty."

I've definitely caught him off guard. His laugh is contagious. "What?"

"I feel like I just had a fling with someone and now I've met back up with my boyfriend." I sigh as I throw the key on the dresser and collapse onto the bed. "Now I sound crazy."

I feel the bed dip and Max lies down next to me. He laughs as he pushes the hair behind my ear. "It's easy to get caught up in all the hype. Don't get lost in the bullshit."

I hear the door click closed and Damien is glaring at the bed. "What's this?"

Max and I laugh. Damien's glare softens. "Calm your shit, D. We're just waiting for you." Max gets up and slaps him in the stomach. "Enjoy my girlfriend."

Damien laughs and grabs for him but Max is faster and gets out of the door before he can touch him. I smile as his attention turns back to me. His blue eyes memorize me. Just a few hours ago I was worried I wasn't strong enough to get involved in a relationship with him. Now, I know that I couldn't give him up if I tried.

He kneels on the floor next to me and pulls me to him. "Hi," he whispers in my ear and goose bumps form all over my skin.

"Hi." I whisper back.

"We've only got a couple hours left. Can I just hold you?" He climbs onto the bed and wraps his arms around me. I can't help but melt into him. "We're back in two weeks. It's only for a weekend but I want to spend it with you if you'll have me. Maybe you can meet Xander?"

"Of course. I'd love that." My eyes burn. Before I know it, the tour will be over and he'll be home. Della handles all of this with such grace. I've decided to take a chapter from her book and not curl up and wait for him to come home. I'm going to enjoy my life until he comes back into it. It's then that I'll truly live. I'm looking forward to that day.

His thumbs caress my face. "You're everything, Mia. I don't ever want to lose us."

My heart hammers in my chest. "I'll be waiting for you."

He kisses my forehead. "I'll get through the next few cities then Joshua will have to end this charade with Oksana. I don't want to hide you. You're not my secret. You're my life."

Tears fill my eyes and all I can do is nod. I know the day we stop hiding will be the best day of my life.

Della takes my hand and smiles at me. I've been dreading the flight home. "It gets easier. I promise. And then before you know it, they're back and you miss your freedom."

"Promise?" Jesus, this woman is gorgeous. It's hard to look away once you've made eye contact.

"You're still in the honeymoon phase. Once it wears off and you realize you can't even breathe when he's home and bored, you'll miss these times. The first tour was hard for me. This one is easier. I guess that it helps we're settled and I have a permanent home in LA." She squeezes my hand before letting go. "When they're home and they aren't recording, they have a hard time being alone. At least Griffin does. He usually has Damien over and they both stare at me like I hold the key to what they're supposed to do with their time off. I'm glad you're around now. Maybe they can both stare at you for awhile."

"It must be such a hardship to have two hot, rock gods staring at you," Laney laughs. "Next time it happens, how about invite a sister over? I need a little more hottie in my life."

"Trust me, it's not glamorous. Both of them in sweatpants, not showered, scratching and groping themselves like they love to do. Add Chance to the mix and it's way too much testosterone in one room. I can feel the hair growing on my chest." Della smiles. "Max is usually my savior. He'll get them out and doing something."

Laney gets the stare down and I can't help but laugh as she squirms. "What?"

"I have an idea." Della claps her hands. "How about asking Max out on a date? He's adorable, Lane. He's a little shy but women like a mysterious man."

"I was thinking the same thing." I beam at her.

"Max is great. But he's not dirty enough for me. I feel like I'd scare him to death." Laney shakes her head no. "What if he's a virgin? I like my boys to be men."

Della chokes on her water. "He's not a virgin. He's had sex with Oksana. I know that for sure. I'm sure they are lots more. But he's not one to kiss and tell." She's quiet for a minute. "He doesn't really ever say much, does he?"

"Oksana sure gets around, doesn't she?" Laney turns back to me. "Where is she?"

"She's walking in some fashion show in New York." Della just shakes her head. "She means well. She's just lost. I just hope someone can find her."

Chapter 15

*Rely on me, let me lead. Take my hand,
you will be freed.
I'd die for you, you are my flesh. Take my
soul and we'll start fresh.
Take the chance, our blood aligned.
The world before us, the past behind. –
Liquid Regret*

I can't wait to see Xander. We've spent the last three days skyping and talking about how life will be different when I'm finally home. We've been back on the road for a week. I miss Mia like mad but I miss him just as much. He's never spent more than a few hours with me. When I'm settled, I'll fight Claire for joint custody. It's time to be a grown up. It's time to settle down, have a family, and finally be a whole person.

Xander has always been a source of joy. It's time I'm the same for him.

"You think she'll like me?" His voice cracks. Puberty is a bitch. I remember every bullshit detail like it was yesterday.

"She already does." I can't help but smile.

"Your dad's whipped." Chance settles in the seat next to me. "But she's hot. You'll be proud of him."

"You landed someone hot?" Xander's question is a joke but it's so convincing, my jaw drops.

Even Joshua laughs. The guys are constantly busting my balls about being a pussy. I really am. I know Harley loves Della but he seems so manly about it. I'm a lovesick puppy. I need a swift kick in the nuts. Just hard enough to dislodge my brain from my dick so I can start thinking like a man.

"We're pulling in to our hotel. We've got two shows in Arizona and a quick trip through Vegas before we head back. Hug your mom."

Xander smiles at me. "Love you, Dad."

My heart absolutely melts every time I hear that. See? Somehow Harley would make that shit sound manly. Me? Nope. I want to squeal like a girl. Christ, I'm losing it.

As the bus stops, I stretch my legs. I'm not going to miss this part of the job. I'm getting tired. I want my car. I want my own shit around me.

"D, text me Mia or Laney's number. Della's not answering her phone. I want to see if they're with her." Harley grabs his bag and heads toward the door. "It's late and I can't find her."

My forehead wrinkles. That's not normal. I shoot Harley the text and dial Mia's number. It goes right to voicemail. I leave her a quick message and follow him off the bus. Joshua is handing out keycards and barking orders at the bellhops. Max is slipping them hundreds and leading everyone into the lobby. It's always chaos until we're inside and behind locked doors.

My phone rings and scares me. Mia's picture stares back at me. "Hey, baby."

"HI." She's giggling and I can hear Laney giving her shit. "I didn't think I'd hear from you tonight. It's late."

"Have you seen Della?" My voice must make her pause. She shushes Laney.

"No. Why?" It's quiet now.

"Griff can't get in touch with her."

"I had a missed call from her a few hours ago. I'll try to call her." She mumbles something to Laney.

"If you can't get her on the phone, could you run by there? I know we're just being paranoid but with everything going on, I'd just sleep better knowing everyone's ok."

"Of course. I'll call you back. Love you, Damien." She hangs up and I instantly miss her.

I take a long shower and order room service. There's nothing on TV. I haven't heard back from Mia and it's been an hour. I crawl under the covers and try to wait her out. My eyes are heavy. I'm losing the battle to stay awake. No news is good news I tell myself as I give in to sleep.

I'm startled awake. I'm completely disoriented. What's that noise? I check my phone but there's nothing. I sit up and take a deep breath. The pounding starts again.

I jump out of the bed and almost rip the door off its hinges. I'm ready to kill whoever's decided to wake me up. One look at Joshua and I'm backing up and letting him in. His eyes are rimmed with red, his face completely void of color.

He points at my bed. "Sit down." His voice cracks. He's in pain.

"What the fuck's wrong?" I can't sit down. I've never seen Joshua like this. "What's happening?"

He takes a deep breath and it shakes. Fuck. I know I should sit. I'm frozen in place. The room is starting to blur. The only thing I can see is Josh struggling to find the words he needs. My hands start to shake as he grabs my arms. He leads me back to the bed and sits. I don't know what else to do so I give in and sit next to him.

"I just got a call from Lex."

My brain is spinning. Lex should be guarding Della. We leave him home because he's the most menacing of the all the security guards we have. Della. He should be guarding Della. Panic sets in. "Fucking say it!" I scream. My voice sounds foreign. I think I know before he says anything else. I can feel it in my bones. Dred is a powerful force. I'm clawing my way out of a black hole, trying to catch my breath. Trying to hear Joshua. Trying to wake up from this nightmare.

A tear runs down Joshua's cheek. I just shake my head no. "He said the girls showed up and wanted to get in the house. He'd been there all night, making rounds. Doing what we fucking pay him to do. He was right fucking there. Outside and didn't know it was happening."

I can't stop shaking my head. I don't know what's happening. I can't make sense of this. "She's ok." I chant it. If I say it enough, it'll be true.

"Laney found her on the kitchen floor. She'd tried to call for help. They tried everything. It was just too late."

I crumple onto the floor. I can't breathe. My tears flood my face and chest. I feel helpless. It's agony.

"Where's Griff?" I need to get to him. I try to stand but my legs give out. Max and Chance are in the doorway. They're just standing there. "Somebody do something." I punch the floor over and over. I can't even feel it. I'm completely numb.

"Stop." Max grabs me and holds me prisoner against him. "You have to stop."

I struggle to get free but it's wasted. He's too strong and I'm completely out of my mind. "Stop fucking holding me down. I need to get to Harley. Get off me."

Chance kneels in front of me and puts his hands on my shoulders.

"We need to tell him together. We're his family. He'll need us."

I crumple to the floor again when Max lets go. My heart is shattered. I know it needs to be me. I'm the one that needs to tell him. He's my family. She's my family. I beg myself to wake up. Please just wake up.

Chapter 16

I can't stop shaking. My hands are covered in blood. The house is full of people. The EMTs have tried to convince me to come with them but I'm too terrified to move. Laney is across from me, wrapped in a blanket. She's crying. Her scream echoes through my head. I'll never forget it.

"Let us in. She's not answering her phone." Laney flirts with Lex and he finally gives in. *"I promise, we won't tell."*

"Did it ever cross your mind that she might not want to talk to you?" Lex smirks when she flips him the bird.

"Let's just make sure she's ok. I want to call Damien and tell him everything's fine." I push past both of them. The house is completely still.

"Of course everything is ok. I've been here all night." Lex flips on the lights in the foyer.

My first thought is how amazing the house is. I'm greeted by granite and hardwoods and big windows. Pictures line the wall leading up to the second floor. Everything is open. It feels like home. My second thought scares me. It's completely silent. There aren't any lights on. Maybe she's not home. She has some girlfriends that she's always going out with.

"She's not home. Now we're just invading her privacy." I shiver. "It's cold in here."

Laney walks through the living room. She's always been a snoop. I turn around and look at Lex. His eyes are wide and he's scanning the doorframe. He turns the deadbolt and pulls but the door stays shut. He pulls the door open and looks at the lock from the outside. I just shrug. Men are weird anyway. Add muscles and a gun and they lose their minds.

Laney's scream rips through the house. It echoes off the walls. I try to run but it's like my feet are stuck in quicksand. Lex shoves past me at a full sprint. When I round the corner, I scream. There's blood everywhere. The white carpet is stained crimson. I can see handprints. I freeze in place.

Lex is yelling at Della to wake up. Laney is staring wide eyed at the kitchen floor. She grabs her phone and dials 911. Her words are frantic. It's like a dream. Everything echoes. Nothing makes sense.

"Don't touch anything!" Lex yells at us and turns his attention back to Della. "God damnit, Del. Wake up."

Like I've been shocked, I jolt awake. I'm moving before I realize it. I run into the kitchen, pushing Laney out of the way. I kneel next to Lex and without saying anything, we start CPR. There's so much blood. Every time I do a chest compression, my hands get soaked. Everything is in slow motion.

The room fills with police, first responders, security guards. Some I recognize, some I don't. Arms wrap around my waist and pull me away from Della's body. I kick and scream trying to get back to her. I can help. She's not gone. I'm carried to the couch by one of the officers. He's asking me questions but I can't hear him. I keep staring at my hands. They're bathed in blood. I wipe them on my pants but I can't get it all off.

I hear the police on their radios. They're calling in the scene. No evidence of forced entry. Multiple stab wounds. I hear them call Della a victim. Dead at the scene. I don't understand any of it. I lean forward and throw up at my feet. My stomach lurches, my head spins. I can hear Laney screaming in the background. Lex is on the phone. I try to speak but my stomach rolls again and I empty what's left onto the carpet.

A female police officer sits with me and wipes blood from my face. She rubs my back and tells me it will be ok. Nothing will ever be ok again.

I look up from my hands and watch them carry Della's body from the house. The house is buzzing with activity. I want to run out of here. I want to wash my hands. The blood is caked dry now.

"Ma'am". I look at the police officer. I didn't realize she was still here.

"We need you to come down to the station with us. We have some questions."

I just nod my head and follow her to the front door. Lex makes eye contact. He's haunted. I know I must look the same. He takes my hand and follows me out the door. Laney is being led out by another officer. I watch as the ambulance pulls away. The lights go on but the siren stays off.

I duck into the back seat of the police cruiser. Lex is right behind me. He puts his arm around me and pulls me to him. I break. The tears won't stop.   My   body   is   shaking uncontrollably. He kisses the top of my head but says nothing. The sound of my crying is the only noise the entire ride. I'm scared. I'm tired. I'm freezing. I want Damien home.

I'm ushered through the station to a small room in back. When Lex tries to follow me, the officer holds up her hand. "We just need to ask her some questions.   I'll let you know when we're finished."

"Not good enough. She's my priority. She's my assignment now. You'll have to let me in with her or we're leaving." Lex is menacing. All six and a half feet of him. The first time I saw him at the concert in LA, he scared the hell out of me. Seeing him tonight is no different.

"I don't understand." I don't know what I could possibly tell the police that would make any difference. I don't need a bodyguard.

"I spoke to Joshua. He wants me with you until they can get back here. We've sent a guard out to Oksana as well. Until we know what happened, we're taking every precaution to keep you both safe."

"I thought Harley was the one being threatened." I wipe my tears away and gag when I realize my hands are still covered.

"He was. We've increased our presence at the hotel. I'm sure he knows by now. Max and Damien are in the spotlight too. We can't take any chances with you or Oksana."

"This can't be happening." I put my head down on the table.

Lex touches my arm and I jump. "I'm sorry. I just want you to know I'm here if you need me."

"I need Damien." I grab for my cellphone but it isn't in my pocket. "Where's my phone?"

"Now isn't the time. Joshua said he was destroyed by the news. We'll get him home to you as soon as we can. Let's just answer their questions and get out of here."

Time stood still. I've heard that phrase a million times in my life. I never knew what it meant until tonight. Nothing feels real. I don't even remember the questions they asked me. Before I knew it, Lex was leading me out to the car the band sent to pick me and Laney up. I had no idea what time it was. I didn't know where we were going. I'm wrapped around Laney. I'm so cold.

The sun breaks over the top of the buildings of the city. I can't even comprehend how a new day has come. Life ended for someone beautiful last night. I don't know how we just go on.

"Where are we going?" Laney's voice breaks.

Lex points to the Hollywood Hills sign. I take the first deep breath I've taken since going into Della's house last night. Even heartbroken and miles away, Damien is making sure I'm safe. "It's ok. We're almost there," I whisper and pull her back into me.

When we pull into the driveway, Steve jogs off the porch to

meet us. He opens the back door and takes me in his arms. He doesn't speak. Just carries me into the house and holds me on the couch as I break in two. Lily is down the stairs and by my side in seconds. The love of my family surrounds me. I've gone through the worst night of my life and they're all here to remind me how much they love me. My eyes are heavy and I rest my head against Steve's chest.

My hands are being cleaned. I don't have the energy to care. I can hear voices. A lot of them. The warm cloth brushes my face. I sigh.

"I'm going to give her something to help her sleep." The voice is angelic. I know I've heard it before. It's one of Lily's friends. I feel a needle stick me in the arm. My eyes roll back and my head swims.

"Steve, grab Laney and take her upstairs. I've got Mia." I'm lifted from the couch.

I force my eyes open. It's hard to focus but the gray eyes that stare back at me are warm. "Kevin." My voice is quiet. I feel like I'm falling into nothingness.

"It's ok. I'm taking you upstairs. We'll all be here when you wake up. Sleep now, doll."

Before I fall into sleep, I smile. My sister has found a life here with Steve and his friends. This house used to belong to Mark Moretti and his wife before Steve bought it for Lil. It's filled with love. It's filled with hope. It's filled with family. I desperately try to hold on to that as my mind turns black and I'm surrounded by nothing.

The last thing I remember before the static is Laney's scream and how I will never be the same.

Chapter 17

Darkness, sorrow, I scream your name
The life that we knew will not be the same.
- Liquid Regret

I stand completely motionless. I'm emotionally and physically drained. I'm about to do the hardest thing I've ever done. As soon as he opens the door, he'll know. There would never be any reason for all of us to show up at his hotel room door in the middle of the night. I tried to convince the others to stay behind but no one thought I could do this on my own. They're probably right.

I can't breathe. I knock on the door praying he won't hear it. I just want to buy a few more seconds. Just a couple. Just enough for them to call and tell me this has all been a huge mistake. It has to be.

I hear the door unlock. My whole life stops. I can tell he's been awake worrying. His eyes meet mine and his face falls. I can't feel my feet but I know I'm moving into his room. It's like being in the middle of a nightmare and praying to wake up. He's just staring at me, shaking his head no. Have I said anything yet? Joshua grabs my arm and I take a deep breath.

"Harley." My voice cracks.

"No." He shakes his head, tears forming in his eyes. "No. No."

"Lex called. I'm so sorry, man. I'm so fucking sorry." I break.

He breaks. He hits his knees, a tortured scream erupts from his throat. It's raw and the most haunting sound I've ever heard. I crawl to him and pull him into my chest. I don't remember anything else. People are talking, the band is all around us. Joshua is on his phone. But I hear nothing. I feel nothing. I'm a black hole, endless, empty.

The tour bus feels like a distant memory. The label sent the jet to pick us up. Our lives are all over the media. I heard the story in the limo, the pilot was whispering about it, Joshua can't get off his fucking phone about it. I want to scream. I want to fight. I want something to numb me. Anything. A pill, a needle, a bottle.

My hands are shaking. I haven't felt this in years. I'm picking at my fingers. It's my old tell and now I can't stop it. They have Harley drugged up. He's crumpled into his chair across from me. I begged them not to use anything on him but he screamed he needed to be numb. It was agony to watch. Not just because I'm scared for him but because I wanted it too. Della was his world. How do you come back from this? How do you get up every morning and keep living?

"The press will be everywhere when we land. They've increased security at the airport. We want to get you through the crowd and to the limos as fast as we can. We need to protect Harley. Cover him with a jacket, surround him. Whatever. Do not let them near him." Joshua doesn't even look up from his phone. I know he's trying to be strong.

"And if we can't wake him up?" Max shakes him a little but Harley barely moves.

"We'll have a guard on each side. We'll carry him if we have to. No pictures of his face. No fuel for their stories." Josh growls.

I just grunt. I want to be home. I want to disappear. I want to wake up and find out this isn't real. I want Mia.

Joshua sits next to me. "We've got a guard on Oksana. I've reassigned Lex to stay with Mia. The police are all over Harley's house. We'll catch who did this."

"What if Harley isn't strong enough? What if I'm not?"

"You both are. I've cancelled the rest of the tour. We'll lay low. The label set up a grief counselor to stay at Max's house with Harley. I suggest you stay there as well." When I shake my head no, Josh continues. "It's not a request. We all need to be together right now. We need to be there for Harley. I've got Oksana set up in the guest house there."

"I don't give a shit about Oksana." I've had enough of this. "I want to see Mia as soon as we land. I'm done with this bullshit. It ends today, Josh."

"No. It doesn't. We'll get Mia to you but this stays secret. We'll deal with that when this blows over. We'll have a press conference about the accident..."

"Accident?" I cut him off. "Bullshit. This wasn't an accident. Somebody did this to her and Lex did nothing?"

"Damien. Calm down. I'm handling this the best I know how. Let's get through this, then we'll talk about Mia. For now, keep your shit together."

If I could kick his ass, I would. I'm not sure I can take him but I'm ready to try. There's so much security on this damn plane that I'd get taken down in a second. We've lost a member of our family. It wasn't an accident. It won't blow over. It won't be behind us. It's a fucking nightmare and it will never end.

When the plane touches down, I see the lines of people, the cameras, the flashbulbs. All the scum of the earth trying to get that shot of Harley's agony that will make them a fortune. My stomach rolls at the thought. I can't comprehend how anyone can justify making money off someone's crisis. I've seen them climb trees, chase us in cars, hide behind corners. They're relentless. My anger is growing. There's one photographer that we trust. One that gets it right. The rest? They thrive off our failures.

"Did you hear me?" Chance touches my arm.

"No. What?" I look at Harley and his eyes are open and emotionless.

"We think it would be best for you to go out first. We'll circle Harley and get him to the cars. They'll want your picture, too. Maybe it will take some of the focus off Griff."

I nod. I'll keep my emotions in check long enough to get to the car. Harley is on his feet, flanked by two guards. His eyes are rimmed in red, his face pale. I've never seen him look like this. Even in all the years of drinking, he's never looked this bad. My heart breaks all over again.

The door opens and I head down the stairs first. I'm blinded by bulbs. People are screaming questions at me. Behind me, I feel the push of the guys getting Harley down the steps. I walk toward the paparazzi and hold my hand up to silence them. It works better than I expect.

"We've cancelled the rest of our tour. We'll hold a press conference with more details but until then, I beg you for privacy." My voice shakes but my face stays vacant. "We've lost someone very close to us."

I feel the tear hit my cheek. Just one. It reminds me this is all real. It's almost in slow motion, reminding me of my pain. I want to wipe it away but in this moment, I feel like it defines me. Let them get the shot. It's not Harley's pain they'll be exploiting. It's something small, but at least it's something I can do.

Security pulls me toward the second limo. The questions start right away but their time is over. They've had enough of us for today. They don't get any more.

Inside, Max nods at me. Just once but it says everything. We'll head to his house. We'll lock the doors and stay until the darkness subsides. It's been eight hours since I found out about Della. It feels like a lifetime ago. There's pain in my chest like someone punched through and ripped my heart right out. It's physical pain. Every breath hurts. My head is pounding. I haven't eaten anything since lunch yesterday. The thought of food makes my stomach roll.

I pull out my cell phone and call Mia. I need to hear her voice.

"Hello?" She's quiet.

"I'm home and I need you." If I say anything else, I'll break down. I hand the phone to Max and let him give her the address. I know he's hurting, too. But there's always been something about Max. A mystery. A secret. Something.

"She'll be there soon, man." Max stares out the window, wounded.

"Thanks," I whisper but he can't hear me.

Was she scared? Did she know it was happening? Did she know who was hurting her? I shiver. Della was like a sister to me. Until Mia, she meant more to me than any woman ever had. She was kind and generous. She was the glue when this group wanted to give up. She was the one who defined coming home for all of us. Her smile lit up a room. Her arms were sanctuary when life got hard. Her laughter was contagious. I'd never hear that again. I'd never feel her hug me. I'd never hear her busting my balls for getting carried away on the road. I'd never be able to call her when I was tempted to fall back into old habits. Life changed last night. It changed forever. It changed for all of us.

Chapter 18

When I got here last night, he was sound asleep. I couldn't wake him. He looked at peace and I knew he wouldn't be if I woke him. Sometime after midnight, he had a nightmare and screamed in his sleep. I held him and he settled. I haven't slept much. The nightmares are intense. I can't imagine what these men are going through. I didn't know Della long but she was amazing and I'm so sad that it hurts.

When he stretches, I smile. I've missed him so much. He opens his eyes slowly and looks at me. He doesn't smile. He pulls me into him and cries. His body shakes and it breaks my heart even more.

"Mia," He whispers.

"Shhh. I'm here. Go back to sleep." I run my hands through his hair and listen to his breathing even out.

I know that there will be a few days of this. I've called into work for the next week. They all think I'm dating Max so there weren't any questions asked. Thank God for that. I don't know how I'll get through the funeral, watching Damien with Oksana, holding onto Max as he grieves. How can I be everything that everyone needs? How can I let myself grieve when I know how much they hurt?

The tap at the door gets my attention. Laney cracks it open and peeks in. "How is he?" She whispers.

I climb out of bed and head to the door. "Still sleeping. How's everyone else?"

"Harley's out cold. Josh is in the kitchen with Chance but I haven't seen Max. How are you holding up?"

"I'm scared." It's not worth it to lie to her. She can see right through me. "Thanks for being here."

"I don't want to be alone." She walks into the living room and sits down. "I've talked to the grief counselor. She's nice. You should talk to her. I think it will help both of us."

"I don't want to leave him for long. I'll find her tomorrow." I can't help but look at the closed bedroom door. "If he wakes up and I'm not there, I won't forgive myself."

She takes my hand. "Mia. Don't talk like that. You lost someone too."

"It's not the same." I wipe the tears from my cheeks. I feel so much guilt. Guilt I didn't get there sooner. Guilt I couldn't get to Damien any quicker. Guilt that if I had answered my phone earlier, maybe this wouldn't have happened.

"It isn't the same." The soft voice catches my attention and I turn around. "Hi Mia. I'm Rachel. You girls went through something that no one can imagine. Something no one should go through. I'm here to talk if you want to."

"I don't know." I instantly shut down.

"I'm here whenever you're ready. I've talked to a couple of the guys and I would love to be able to talk to you too."

"Ok." The bedroom door opens and I'm instantly on my feet.

Damien rubs his eyes and gives us all a sad smile. "I woke up and you weren't there. I missed you."

I know he's heartbroken but he still takes my breath away. "I'm sorry."

"Sit back down. I need to get out of that room." He hugs me and I instantly feel better. "Hey, Laney. How's Harley?"

"I only talked to him for a minute but I doubt he'll remember. He's been asleep all night though." Laney hugs him and then hugs me. "I'm going to find something to eat. I'll cook something for all of us. I'm sure you guys must be getting hungry."

Laney and Rachel head to the kitchen and I'm left alone with Damien. I'm so nervous. I don't want to say the wrong thing, do the wrong thing. I just stand here frozen. I feel helpless.

"Thanks for being here." Damien pulls me into his lap and kisses my neck. "I need to hold you."

"I love you." I kiss him lightly. "I'll stay as long as you need me to."

His hand slips up the back of my nightgown and pulls me against him. His kiss deepens. He bites at my bottom lip and I can feel him harden under me. He runs his hands down my back and cups my ass. When he moves my hips against him, there's no turning back. We both need this.

"Fuck me, Mia." He growls into my ear. "Make me forget."

I pull at his sweatpants and his erection springs free. I lick my lips. He's got the most beautiful body. A drop of pre come seeps from the tip and I run my finger across it and lick it clean. His eyes darken. He reaches under my nightgown and yanks my panties aside. There's no foreplay tonight but we don't need it. We're both ready and need to get lost in each other.

He sinks into me, his cock hot and hard. I don't care who might walk in or who might be watching. I circle my hips and watch him lie his head back against the couch cushions. He hisses when I lift almost all the way off and then slam back down onto him.

"Again." He moans.

I do it again and his eyes shut completely. I pull at his hair and his hips thrust forward. I've had him rough and I've had him gentle. Every time is better than the last. The sounds he makes turn me on more than anything in the world. When he takes control, I'm lost.

Every thrust of his hips hits me in just the right spot. I'm soaked. I'm horny. I need to come. I grab my nipples and roll them in between my fingers and my thumbs. My head falls back. The friction mixed with his strong pumps make it almost too intense.

"I love getting lost in this hot pussy. I love feeling you drip down my cock." He grabs my hips and pounds into me. His voice is broken with each stroke. "You. Make. Me. So. Fucking. Hard."

"Oh God." I grab at his shoulder, the couch cushions, anything that can anchor me. I'm so close. I can feel it building. I can feel the tingle start.

"Let go, baby. Let me feel you drench me." He bites my nipple and I explode around him. My whole body convulses in pleasure.

"Fuck." He runs his fingers through my orgasm and wipes it onto my nipple. His lips suck it off, hard. I tighten around him and a second wave hits. He erupts, filling me, soaking his lap.

I fall into his chest, gasping, my body still shivering around his. I never want this to end. When we're together, everything is right with the world. I feel incredibly satisfied. I know I'm lucky. It's never been like this with anyone.

After a few minutes, dread creeps back in. We hold each other as tightly as we can. I know we need to face what's happened but denial is very powerful when you lose someone. For the first time in twenty-four hours, I could close my eyes without seeing Della.

I lean up and look into his eyes. He's haunted. "I'm so sorry, Damien. I'm so, so sorry."

He shakes his head but doesn't say anything. His eyes fill with tears but he holds them back. He kisses me gently, then stands up with me still wrapped around him.

He carries me into the bedroom, leaving discarded clothes in the living room. Setting me down gently, he tucks my hair behind my ear. His hands cup my face and he takes a deep breath. "I don't know what to do. I don't know what to say to Harley. I just want to lock the door and not let anyone else in."

"I know." I rub my hands up and down his arms. "No one expects you to have any answers. Just be here for him. That's all you can do."

"Ok." He just stares at me.

"Come on. Let's shower and get something to eat. Then we can lock the world out for the rest of the night."

I lead him into the bathroom and start the shower. Once the water is warm, I pull him in and lather up a wash cloth. He lets me wash him, watching my every move. He's quiet and wide eyed. He says I saved him once. I want to do it again. I want to heal him. I want him to forget for a while.

He starts to harden under my touch. I take him into my mouth, circling the sensitive tip, swallowing when he hits the back of my throat. His hands shoot out and brace himself on the tile. Our eyes lock as I suck him, slowly, gently, taking all my cues from him. He takes control, moving in and out of my mouth. When he stops, I suck hard and moan. His knees nearly buckle.

He pulls me from the floor and lifts me. Wrapping my legs around him, he pins me against the shower wall. His lips find mine, our tongues dance. His taste is fresh on my tongue and pushes my desire up a notch. As he pushes into me, he watches my face. I get lost in his endless, blue eyes. His strokes are slow, passionate. He kisses me every few seconds.

"I love you, Mia. I love you so much." He rests his forehead against mine. "I would be lost without you."

His fingers find my clit and I come apart, my eyes never leaving his. He smiles knowing he's the only one in the world that makes me feel this way. He's my fairytale. He just redefines Prince Charming. I wouldn't have it any other way.

Chapter 19

We interrupt this tour to bring you a moment of silence to remember one of our own. – Liquid Regret

The morning of the funeral is rainy and cold. I used to love the fall in California when the sunny days turned breezy and the nights got colder. Today, it's like even God is in mourning. Clouds cover the sky, the rain falling like tears against the sidewalk. Thunder rolls, echoing our anger at a life lost way too soon. The wind whips so hard, bringing with it the sting of loss.

My suit feels too tight. I pull at my tie to try to loosen the collar and let me breathe easier. Despite the cold, my hands are sweating. I'm praying the media is kind today. There's no way to prevent the circus outside the funeral home. We all know that. But if I get one wish today, it's that their words are filled with love for the beautiful person we all lost.

Harley is stoic. Oksana has been a rock for him and I appreciate that. I can actually see some good in her and it makes her much more tolerable. Max is quiet. He has been for the few days we've been home. Chance has handled this better than all of us. He's been able to make the plans for not just today, but the days after that will inevitably lead us back out on tour. Joshua has stepped up and taken control of the media and what stories get told. The stories have mostly been positive and I'm thankful for that. Seeing Della's image ruined in the media would push us all over the edge.

As we pull up to the funeral home, the mood is somber. The media is lined up for pictures but there's sadness in the air. The stories and images that Joshua has provided them with have made Della look like the superhero she was.

Stepping from the limo, the flashbulbs go off. There are questions asked but we're able to get Harley inside before much damage is done. Chance stays behind for questions while we head inside and get ready to say our final goodbyes.

"I can't do this." Harley's voice cracks. "I don't know how to fucking do this."

My arm goes around him and he leans into me. I'll be his rock. I can grieve later. He's my family and there's no one that needs me more than he does. "We'll do it together."

"She was everything. She was forever." Tears fill his bloodshot eyes.

"I know, man." I make sure he gets to the front row before I take the seat next to him. My arm rests on the back of his seat. I'm trying to wrap him in strength. Strength I don't have. Strength I desperately need.

Oksana stops at the end of the row and looks at us. "Can I sit in between you?"

"Why don't you sit on the other side of Harley?" Joshua whispers and points to the seat on his other side. Part of me questions it but the other is relieved I can stay near him, feeding off his love for Della. "Mia's here and she wants to sit with you."

Mia gives me a sad smile before taking the seat next to me. I know what a risk Josh is taking having us out in public like this. I'll never be able to thank him for letting it go, just for today. Her fingers curl through mine and I'm instantly grounded. My heart slows, my shoulders relax. I notice Max sitting at the end of the row and he gives her a wink. I squeeze her hand, just making sure she's real.

As the pastor takes his place at the front of the room, Harley crumples into me. Seeing him so broken is like getting the wind knocked out of me. I tighten my grip on his shoulder and let him use me to stay upright.

"Thank you for coming. Please be seated. My name is Scott Simpson. I'm the pastor of Liberty Hills Presbyterian Church. It's with a heavy heart that I am in front of you today. Della Barron Miles meant the world to so many of us. Her heart was as big as any I've known. I had the honor of meeting Della a few years ago while she was doing volunteer work for the homeless shelter. Her enthusiasm was contagious. Her love for others was apparent in everything she did. She was a familiar face at Sunday service when she was in town. I was blessed to officiate her wedding when she married the love of her life. The love she had for Griffin was rare. Through everything, she smiled and had faith it would be alright. She was certainty your biggest cheerleader."

Harley lets out a silent sob as the pastor goes on to tell the congregation about the journey of love she took by Griff's side. He told stories that made us smile. He told stories that made my soul hurt. His favorite memory was one of her dancing in the rain with the rest of us when one of our outdoor shows got rained out. I'd forgotten about that day.   Remembering her laugh, the reflection of love in her eyes every time she looked at one of us, makes the tears stream down my face. There's no use in trying to prevent them.   I've lost someone who was ripped from my life far too early.

When the pastor is finished, we all have a chance to tell stories. The mood is light and we're smiling and laughing through the heartache. Chance is first and of course, he has us laughing about the time he hit on Della and didn't realize she was Harley's 'old lady'. Josh tells us about meeting Della for the first time and how she refused to let him say no to a contract with us. I always wondered how it had been so easy to get the hottest name in the agency. Della was a pit-bull when it came to us. Hearing the story warms my heart. I send a silent prayer of thanks to her.

Max is next. His tall frame leans against the altar, bending into the microphone. "I didn't find these guys. Della found me. I had left home and didn't have anywhere to go. I was sitting in the park, a day a lot like today, hiding under an umbrella and scribbling in a notebook. I was writing a song and tapping out the rhythm on my jeans. She sat down next to me and took the book from my hands. Didn't say a word. Just stole it. I think I just sat there with my mouth open. I couldn't say anything. She was the most beautiful woman I'd ever seen. After she read some of it, she sang it back to me and let me hear it. She was this tiny person, soaking wet from the rain, just smiling at me. I knew I'd met someone special. She invited me back to the apartment she shared with Harley and Damien. We ate hotdogs,

I think. Then she made us all play the song I had written."

Max wipes his eyes and then smiles the most genuine smile I've ever seen from him. "I fell in love with her. I'm not sure you knew that, Griff."

Harley laughs. "We both did."

"It was an honor to love her. She was the most amazing person I've ever known. I've prayed for someone like her to come into my life. Now I pray that she watches over all of us and helps us find our way. I know we have an angel on our side, someone who won't let us lose who we are and where we're going."

I stand on shaking legs and slowly walk to the microphone. The room is packed with familiar faces. Fans, friends from her work, family members we haven't seen in years. She made a difference in the lives of every person in this room. I take a deep breath and allow myself to get lost in Mia's eyes.

"I was in a really dark place when I met Della and Griff. They became my family the first night we met. They welcomed me into their life together like I was always meant to be there. It was the three of us against the world. Dell called us the tripod that held the weight of the world. She believed we could do anything together. I used to laugh at her but I think she was right. The last few days, it's been really hard to keep things together with a piece of that tripod missing. Nothing seems balanced anymore. I look at Harley and I wonder how the hell I'll hold things together for both of us."

I wipe at my eyes and smile at Griff. He smiles back, love and heartbreak written all over his face. "Dell was the person I called when everything got really hard. If I had a problem I couldn't solve or had the urge to throw away my sobriety, she would talk to me like a person. No blame. No disappointment. Just love. She'd tell me 'D, the past doesn't define you unless you let it.' She was also the person I turned to when I couldn't get rid of a woman after a night on tour. Oh shit. Sorry Pastor." My eyes widen and I laugh.

Harley laughs from the front row and it makes me feel better. Joshua just shakes his head and smiles. Even Mia giggles. "She'd come in and act like a possessive girlfriend. Anything it took to get rid of them. That's when I got to see crazy Della and trust me, she was a little scary. Then she'd smack me in the back of my head and yell at me. She was like a sister. A pain in my ass. She would sneak out at midnight and eat my leftovers. If I was saving something, it's like she had radar and would always steal it. She used all my shampoo. She left shit everywhere in the bathroom. She stuck her nose in my business every second. She had an opinion on everything. She was perfect. I would do anything to take her place. I would give up everything to have her back. I've never lost anything as valuable as her. The pain is something I won't ever forget. Della, if you can hear me, I promise you that I'll take care of Griff. I promise that I'll live my life in a way that will make you proud. I love you, Dell."

When I sit back down, Harley hugs me. "Thank you. You meant

everything to her too. She loved you, D."

Mia takes my hand and brings it to her lips. She kisses my fingers and lets me fall into her a little more. I'm not sure I'll survive this but if I do, it will be because of the beautiful redhead that has stolen my heart.

Chapter 20

Watching Damien pour his heart out about Della makes me fall even more in love with him. He's raw and instead of shutting down, he's wide open to the pain of losing her. Hearing Harley laugh eases my pain. I didn't know Della long but I know she made an impact on me in that short period of time.

I hold onto Damien's hand like a lifeline. I know he thinks I'm doing it to help him. But honestly, it's for me. Being able to love him is what makes me whole. It's what gives me strength. It's what helps me find peace in this tragedy.

Harley makes his way to the front of the room. He's stronger than I'll ever be. He's gathered strength from everyone in the room and used it to help him find the courage to share his feelings about Della. His bravery is what makes him who he is.

"Della would be happy to see so many people she loved in one room. I wish it could've been for a different reason. I'd give my life for hers if I could. Hers was a lot more valuable." Harley takes a deep breath and stays quiet for a minute before continuing. "I've loved Della my whole life. I honestly don't remember anything before her. I loved her the first second I saw her. I can't imagine loving anyone else the way I do her. I know I never will again. She lived her life for everyone else. She dedicated every free second to making sure someone else was happy. I'd always sit back and watch her, just in awe of who she was. She could've been anything she wanted to be. She could've had anyone in the world. But she chose me. Me. With all my demons and all my flaws. She told me none of that mattered because her heart had found its other half. She never judged me. I tried so many times to get sober and every single time I failed, she just picked me up and helped me start over. Who does that? Who honestly gives someone so many chances and doesn't walk away?"

My heart breaks as Harley starts to cry. His beautiful face is shadowed in agony, every tear representing a minute of time he won't ever have with Della. He's a completely broken man. A shell of who he was when we flew to Seattle. My heart breaks for him. My whole body hurts for him. I want to make everything better for him. I want him to know Della would be proud of how he's handled the hardest time in his life. I want to do anything to help. I just don't know what to do, what to say. Words will never be enough.

He gathers his composure. "I'm so mad that I wasn't home to save you, baby. I can't imagine a world where anyone would want to hurt you. I promised that I'd protect you and I didn't. I was on the tour bus, laughing, writing music and you were taking your last breath. I don't know how I'll live my life without you. I don't know how I'll forgive myself enough to keep going. But I make a promise to you, in front of all the people we love, that I'll find out who did this to you. I'll never stop looking. They took the person that mattered more to me than anyone in the world. I may be standing here breathing but they took my life when they took yours. Things will never be the same. I will make sure they pay for what they did to you. What they did to all of us. I love you, Della."

Harley walks to her casket and puts his hand on the top. His tears are silent. "To cherish and keep you, to be faithful and true, to love you and honor you, forsaking all others til death do us part. This isn't goodbye, sweetheart. It's just see you soon. It's what you said every time I got on that bus. You will always be my wife. You will always have my heart. No matter where I go, you will be with me."

Damien drops my hand and stands up. He walks to Harley and hugs him. He whispers to him before putting his hand next to Harley's on the casket. Max and Chance are right behind him. They share a moment together, saying goodbye in the only way they know how.

Damien's voice is quiet. "Dell loved country music. For her last birthday, she asked us to play a song by Rascal Flatts while we were onstage. She loved anything sad. We didn't share her taste in music but when Della asked for something, you did it. Her favorite song was Here Comes Goodbye. I'm not sure I'll get through this but I have to try."

I want to hold him. I want to hold him so he knows he isn't alone. Sitting here, watching the four most beautiful men in the world letting go of something so special is tearing me in two. Oksana is crying a few seats away. Her body shakes as she watches the men get ready to sing their goodbye to Della. She's pale and her eyes are red. I move to sit next to her. She's startled at first but takes my hand anyway. In another world, we may have been friends. She's lost and Della was always able to see the best in her. It's time for me to try too. Della fought for her. Now it's my turn.

Chance plays the melody to Here Comes Goodbye. His fingers move like they are dancing over the strings. The song is haunting. I haven't heard it before and listening to the words is tough. It's a beautiful melody, full of heartbreak and loss. Damien's voice is strong, even if he isn't. Every time I hear him sing, I get swept away. Today is no different.

"I'm glad Damien has you." Oksana's voice is a whisper but it's enough to pull me out of my Damien daydream.

"I'm glad he has you too." I smile at her.

As the song finishes, Joshua and Lex join the men as they carry the casket to the waiting hearse. I hold onto Oksana as we are led out in front of the rest of the guests. Eyes lock on us, making me feel on edge. I can hear the shutters of cameras. I hear whispers and can only imagine what the media will say about us. Will I be the other woman? Will I be the supportive friend? It doesn't matter to me now. The only thing on my mind is helping Damien and the rest of the band get through the burial and get back to Max's house where we are safe and away from the spotlight.

Joshua takes my hand and leads me and Oksana to the second limo. Everything happens so fast that I don't realize we're even closed in the car until Oksana hands me a bottle of water.

"You get used to it. It's hard to ignore it at first but pretty soon it'll feel normal. I'm not sure if that's a good thing or not." Oksana digs through her purse and pulls out a pill bottle. She swallows one and looks back at me. "Anxiety."

I just nod. I know her story. I've heard it from Damien and again from Della. "It's a hard day."

"Someone that understands. Cheers." She clinks her water bottle against mine. "I was so devastated when I got the news. I'd just gotten home from New York that night. I was sound asleep and there was a guard pounding on my door. Said Joshua had hired him to protect me and told me what happened to Della. I was terrified I could be next. How did you hear?"

"We found her." I look out the window and try not to relive it. "Lex stayed with me until I got to Max's house the next night."

Oksana leans forward and whispers, "What do you think Lex was doing when she was getting stabbed? Do you really believe he didn't hear anything?"

"I don't know. I really don't want to talk about it." I'm not sure how I ended up in this limo with just Oksana and a bodyguard. "It's a scene I'm having a hard time getting out of my head."

"You poor thing. I can't imagine seeing that. She was a good person. Do you think Harley will ever get over her? I think they need to take a closer look at Lex. He was the only one there. The only one that had access to her."

The bitch is certifiable. What part of I don't want to talk about it does she not understand? I take a deep breath. "I think Lex is a good man. I feel safe when he's around."

"Maybe you shouldn't. You never know who you can trust. I just think it's strange that the person who was hired to keep her safe didn't see anything. He says he was making rounds. Don't you think he would have heard something? You can't tell me she didn't scream. She had to scream. I can't image the pain she must have felt. Do you think she knew she was going to die? She had to scream for Lex to help her. He'll have to live with that."

"Oksana." My voice is harsher than I expected. It makes her jump. "I can't talk about this. Please, stop."

She digs through her purse again. Her whole demeanor has changed. Whatever she took has kicked in. Even the look on her face is different. I take a few deep breaths, reminding myself that Della would help her if she was here. She looks out the window, lost in a narcotic haze.

The limo stops and we get out. The sun has broken through the clouds, a ray of light shining down on all of us. I follow people toward the tent where the final portion of the funeral will take place. The men carry the casket to where she'll be buried. They're all composed, here with us but somewhere else in thought.

The pastor says a final prayer and they lower Della's body into the ground. I wipe the tears from my cheeks, unable to take a full breath. The whole service is beautiful. The stories were full of love, the emotions were real and shared by everyone. I know that somewhere Della is smiling down at all of us, giving us strength and helping us make it through the day.

As the crowd begins to say their goodbyes, a breeze blows, making everyone stop and smile. I shiver knowing something greater is happening. The sun's rays shine onto our portion of the cemetery, warming our skin and reminding us that we're alive.

Harley smiles at the sky. "I love you too, baby."

Chapter 21
Take my hand, show me the way.
Lead me to love and beg me to stay.
— Liquid Regret

I can't sleep. Every time I try, I dream about losing Mia. It's Mia that's gone and I can't breathe. It's the third night in a row. It started the night of the funeral and I can't handle much more. It's selfish to feel this way. I feel so fucking guilty that I'm happy I didn't lose the love of my life.

"You ok?" Mia curls into my side and yawns. "You've been talking in your sleep again."

I flip the light on and sit up. "It's time to tell Joshua I'm done playing the game."

"What?" She's so beautiful when she first wakes up.

"If Della's death taught me anything, it's that life's too short. I can't live this lie with Oksana anymore. I can't put my life on hold. I want the world to know that I love you. I can't do this anymore."

She bites her bottom lip. Any time she's nervous, she starts chomping on that lip. It always makes me hard. I want to bite it. I want to pull it into my mouth and taste her. "I just don't want you to regret it."

I roll on top of her and suck her lip into my mouth. Her whimper is such a turn on. "The only thing I regret is living the lie in the first place." I lick my way up her jaw and stop at her ear. When I whisper, goose bumps break out all over her arms. "I want to be with you every second of every day."

My tongue traces the vein in her neck. I can feel her heartbeat hammering and I smile knowing I can do this to her. She's the most beautiful woman on the planet and she's all mine. I kiss my way along her collarbone and her back arches, pressing her gorgeous tits into me.

Her fingers find the waistband of my boxers. She's greedy when she's turned on. She's always so ready for me. I'm a lucky son of a bitch. Her knees fall open, giving me full access to the promise land. My fingers run across the silk of her panties. She's already soaked.

There's no time to take anything off. I need to be inside her. I push my boxers down and pull the scrap of fabric away from her beautiful pussy. I need to show her what she does to me. I need her to feel how hard she makes me. I push into her in one deep stroke, her hungry body taking everything I've got.

"Fuck." Her walls are hot, wet, ready to take every drop of pleasure from me. "I love feeling you soak my cock."

I roll onto my back and pull her on top. Her body moves in sync with mine. She pulls her hair out of her ponytail, letting the waves of silk fall around her shoulders. She's a goddess. Her hair runs over her nipples, causing them to harden. When she pinches them, I swear I almost come.

"Fuck me. Take everything you need. Ride my cock, baby."

Her eyes hood at my words. Her hips start a punishing rhythm, pounding against my erection, making me want to explode. The sound of our bodies slapping together is music to my fucking ears. She's drenched, soaking my balls and she hasn't even come yet.

Her head falls back and I know she's close. I can feel her swelling, almost pushing me out of her body. I reach forward and flick her clit and that's all she needs. There's a rush of hot liquid and I need to taste her.

I throw her off of me, yanking her legs over my shoulders and burying my face between her thighs. Her flavor explodes on my tongue. I can't get enough. I lick and suck until there's nothing left. Even then it's not enough.

"I'm hungry, baby. You're going to come over and over again until I've had my fill."

She screams my name when I bite her clit. My fingers find her G-spot and she explodes again. When my tongue licks her juices from her gorgeous pussy, she grabs my hair and rides my face. It's the most erotic feeling in the world. I can hardly breathe but I can't think of a better way to go out. Suffocation by pussy.

"I'm so close, Damien. Yes. Yes."

Her whole body goes rigid right before she shatters. My face is soaked. My bed is soaked. I'm hard as steel and need to fuck her. Hard.

"I need to fuck you." I hardly recognize my own voice. I'm so turned on I can't think straight. This won't take long. My balls are pulled up tight against my body. I'm ready to explode.

I shove into her, my lips crashing onto hers. We're both out of breath. Our tongues slide over each other, sucking, fucking each other with our mouths. We're both so close to orgasm that I'm not sure who'll let go first. It's a race to the finish. I want her to win but I'm a selfish son of a bitch and I need to come right now more than I need to breathe.

My body moves against hers. Every time I hit her favorite spot, she cries out my name. I pull her up as close as I can so that my body rubs against her clit. Her nails scratch my back, breaking the skin and I couldn't give a fuck. I can feel the tingle race down my spine.

Mia's back arches and she screams. Her orgasm pulls me over and I explode, emptying every drop into her. I keep moving until we both come down from the most intense lovemaking we've ever had. I plan on doing this a couple more times tonight. Her body is my obsession. I won't ever let go.

Max is sitting in the living room, staring right through the TV. Before I tell Joshua anything, I need to know the guys are behind me. Chance looks up from his phone when I sit down. I'm not sure where Harley is but I already know he'll have my back.

"I need to talk to you guys." I watch as Max shifts his eyes to me. "I want to come clean about Oksana. I don't want to hide Mia anymore. It's not fair to her or Oksana. I need to know you're ok with all of it. I don't want to do anything that will be bad for the band."

"Go for it, man. I didn't get the big deal from the beginning. Screw the label. Be happy." Chance looks back down at his phone. "There's always another gig."

"Max?" I hold my breath waiting for his answer.

"How does Mia feel about all this?"

"She wants to be honest. But she'd never do anything to hurt you guys." It's the honest truth.

"Then do it. You don't need our permission. Whatever happens, we're a family. We've got your back."

"And if you're in the line of fire for going along with the bullshit?" My biggest fear is that Max will face a shit storm for getting involved in my fuck ups. If the label lets me go, I'll be ok. I would rather be with Mia than let them run my life. But letting Max take the fall won't sit well with me.

"Dude, Mia's cool. She's good for you. Everything changed when she showed up. Let them say whatever they want. We know the truth. Fuck 'em." Max shrugs his shoulders.

Max is a mystery. He doesn't usually say much. But when he does, its genius. Chance usually says too much, digging a deeper hole that he has to climb out of. Both of them are on my side and willing to fight this battle with me.

I've known from the beginning that Mia would win. It's obvious to everyone that I'm a better person with her by my side. It was never a question that I'd pick her. It was just a matter of timing. Us against the world. The ticking time bomb that Joshua was trying to keep hidden.

I grab my cell phone from my pocket and dial his number. He picks up on the second ring. "Hey, man. We need to talk."

I listen to him take a deep breath. He knows what's coming. I don't need to say anything else. His voice is tired. It's been a wild ride the last few months. We're all exhausted.

"Do what you need to do, Damien. I'm on your side."

His words are what I needed to hear. This ends tomorrow.

Chapter 22

The beach has always been my sanctuary. Being at Max's house this week has been heaven. The steps off the back of the house lead down to a secluded area of beach that looks practically untouched. I've snuck down here every night. No, it's not smart. But I can't help myself. I need to get away from all the sadness. I feel like I'm getting sucked into a black hole of nothingness and if I let myself fall in, I'll never climb out.

I sit in my usual spot. A tiny stump stuck in the sand where my toes can dig in and feel the water's caress. It's my little piece of heaven in the hell that we're living in. The waves roll onto the shore, soothing my broken heart. The breeze allows me some deep breaths. I wonder if Della is looking down on us.

The days since the funeral have been a struggle. Damien talks about her with me. Sometimes we laugh and sometimes we cry. She was a special person and I'm blessed that I've gotten to see how deeply her love touched Damien and the rest of the band. They've been writing again. The songs are beautiful and I can feel her spirit in the house when the music starts.

"Mind if I sit?" Harley's voice startles me. He chuckles when I grab my chest. "Sorry, kiddo. Didn't mean to scare you."

"Have a seat." I pat the stump next to me. "I could use the company."

Harley sits and looks out over the water. He smiles. "Della loved it out here. When we were looking for our house, we stayed here for a few weeks. This was her favorite spot. She'd sneak down here almost every night. Drove Lex crazy even then."

"I can see why. It's nice out here. The rest of the world just kind of fades away when I'm out here." I smile when he takes my hand.

"She loved you. The first time she met you, she said Damien would be nuts to let you get away. They talked about you for hours. I gave him so much shit about it. I'd give anything to hear them again." He shakes his head and takes a deep breath in through his nose. He sighs when he lets it out. "You're good for him. I know things haven't been ideal with the media and the security detail and all the other bullshit. I hope you'll hang in there. I think we all need a woman around right now."

I lean into him as he wraps his arm around me. "I don't plan on going anywhere. I love him. I don't think I could walk away now if I wanted to."

"That's good." He's lost in thought for a long time. I sit with him in the silence and watch the water. It's therapeutic.

When he shivers, I can't help but ask. "How are you doing, Harley? I'm really sorry about everything."

He nods his head and his eyes fill with tears. "I want a drink. Every minute is a struggle. I want something to make me numb. Something to take the pain away. Then I remember Della's face the night I got my one year chip at AA. I'd been so close, so many times and I'd finally done it. She's not here to pick me up anymore. I need to remember her face. I need to figure out how to still be alive when she isn't."

I pull him into a hug and let him fall apart. "It's one minute at a time. One breath at a time. It's all we can do. We just need to keep moving ahead and figure it out as we go. No one has the right answer. If you get lost, just ask her the way."

He holds me so tightly that it's hard to breathe. I don't dare move. I can only imagine that this is the safest he's felt since he got the news. I haven't seen him let anyone hold him. I rub his back as he sobs in my arms. I hear the guys calling for us from the porch. It's dark down here and I'm not sure they can see us. It doesn't matter anyway. There's nowhere else I'd rather be in this moment. As Harley takes his first step toward healing, I take one toward being a part of this family. We will take this journey together. Whatever it takes, we'll all get there together.

I feel Damien's hand on my shoulder. I don't need to open my eyes to know it's him. My body would recognize him anywhere. He's home for me. He pulls both of us into his arms and holds us. I take my strength from him and give it all to Harley. It's a gesture I know they've shared with Della. She told me about all the times she held them both when Harley would fall off the wagon again. It was a gesture of love and that's exactly what it is for me now.

Harley pulls away first and wipes my tears. "Thank you. I needed that more than you know."

He stands and looks up at the sky. It's a private moment between him and Della. It's beautiful and heartfelt. When it's over, he walks away and doesn't look back. I watch him leave. He takes a piece of me with him. I hope it will keep him strong.

I woke up alone this morning. Damien told me he had something he needed to do with the guys and gave me a day to sleep in. It's back to work tomorrow. It will be hard to get back into a routine. I know as each day passes, we're one day closer to saying goodbye again. The rest of the tour dates have to be rescheduled and it's where they belong.

I stretch and smile. My body is sore in all the right places. I've spent the last few nights making love to

Damien. Neither of us needs sleep. I'll sleep when they're on the road. For now, I want to enjoy every minute we have.

He says he's ready to tell the world about his engagement to Oksana and why the story was started in the first place. It scares me that he'll look like a villain while she looks like a victim. She plays the role so well. I've tried to talk to her a few times since the funeral. We have nothing in common. Every conversation is forced. She's way too comfortable living in the guest house. I don't see her leaving any time soon. When she's not all over Chance, she's fawning all over Harley. It makes me sick to my stomach.

I growl as I get out of bed. She's sucked so much of my energy just being in the same space. I giggle when

I think about Damien coming clean about the whole charade. Where will that leave her?

Laney comes crashing through my bedroom door and I scream. She runs at the nightstand and grabs my phone. "I've been calling you. Turn on the TV."

"You scared the shit out of me. How'd you get in here?"

"Harley's home. Turn on the fucking TV." She's looking for the remote.

"Alright. Jesus. Calm down." I grab the remote off the bed and aim at the TV. When it flicks to life, Damien's face fills my screen. "What the hell?"

Laney sits down on the bed and claps her hands. "Turn it up."

Harley comes in to see what's happening. He laughs when he sees the screen. He sits on the bed next to Laney and puts his arm around her. "What's up, Lane?"

"Shut up. Both of you." Her eyes are locked on the screen.

I can't believe what I'm hearing. It's like I'm in a dream. When I hear Oksana scream from the other room, I want to dance. It's finally happening.

Chapter 23

The lies stop here, the truth takes flight.
I'll take the chance and do what's right.
— Liquid Regret

I can't believe I'm about to do this. Max gives me courage just by sitting next to me. The lights seem hotter than usual. I'm a pro at press conferences by now but this one has me on edge. My career, and the success of the band, depends on everything I say right now.

I clear my throat and that's all they need. Cameras go off, reporters shove tape recorders a little closer, trying to be the first to get the scoop. I know they all assume this is about Della. But, it isn't. I've made a deal with myself that I will keep living. She'd want that for me. She'd kick my ass if she thought I wasn't going to fight to do what's right. I can feel her with me and she's pushing me to love Mia the way I need to. Not the way the label thinks it should happen.

"Thank you all for coming today. I know this is last minute. We've had a lot to deal with the past few weeks and this is my first step toward healing. Della was my family. She was the one I'd turn to with just about anything. Her death made me open my eyes and realize how short life is and if I don't take the chances I want to, it may be too late. A few months ago, my name was all over the tabloids. I'd lost my way and made some really bad decisions. I was stupid. I take full responsibility for all of my actions. I apologize to anyone that may have been hurt by my carelessness. One of those women was Oksana, who is probably watching this right now and imaging all the ways she's going to kill me when I get home."

I chuckle when Max starts laughing. He knows her as well as I do. I know this is kind of a douche move. A sneak attack of sorts. But I've talked to her over and over and she isn't willing to let this charade go. I'm going to try to make her look like a saint when I'm done today. I just hope I don't make myself look like an asshole.

"My career was heading down the toilet and I was the one doing the flushing. Oksana has a big heart and I used that for personal gain. She needed me as much as I needed her. We were two lost souls looking for anything to grab on to. She threw me a lifeline and I ran with it. The story of us being engaged was created by the powers that be. I was honored to stand at her side. In another lifetime, maybe that's where I would be today. Who knows? We might have made a great team. But the story of our engagement was just something that was thrown out there to try and save me from throwing my life away. I will never be able to thank Oksana enough."

The media is buzzing. The bomb I just dropped rips through the crowd. The questions start immediately. Everyone is yelling over each other in an attempt to get their questions answered first. Max holds up his hand to calm everyone down. When they settle, I continue.

"The other person this rumor hurt was a woman who means the

world to me. Before we headed out on our first tour, I met someone. She was everything I wanted, everything I needed. I let her get away then but I'm not willing to do that again. She saved me from everything in my life that was dark. We reunited a few months ago and I fell even harder. If Harley was up here saying these things, he'd sound really cool. I just sound like a complete sap but I'm ok with that. Mia means more to me than anything in the world and I couldn't live another minute without her by my side. I was having a hard time being away from her so Max stepped in and took his part in this big disaster of a lie and kept her close to us. Just knowing she was close was enough for me. She and Max would appear together in public and I would stand by Oksana and it was supposed to make everything ok. But, it didn't."

The cameras are pointed at Max now and he just smiles like the champ he is. I will never be able to repay him for what he's done for me. "Max had to put his life on hold because I had fallen in love with a woman that I had to keep hidden from the world. Thank you for that, man. I couldn't have made it through the past few weeks without her or without you."

Max shakes my hand. "I'd do it again if it meant you were happy."

That got them. The women in the room have officially swooned over Max Callum. His moment in the spotlight is just beginning. He's stolen the hearts of the world with one sentence. Bastard.

"When Della was alive, we spent hours talking about my relationship with Mia and how I needed to come clean about the

Oksana engagement. She told me that Mia was the one and I'd be crazy if I did anything to let her get away. She said it every day. I would just smile like a lovesick puppy. I couldn't help myself. Now that she's gone, I need to honor her memory by being truthful with all of you. And being truthful with myself. I need to let Max live his life and not have a responsibility to me. I need to let Oksana take her career back and travel and live. She's gorgeous and one hell of a model and I know success will follow her wherever she goes. I need to apologize to my label, and to all of you that I've wronged, for being so unpredictable and not giving a second thought to who my actions hurt. I apologize to my agent for putting you in a position where you had to clean up my mess. More than once."

Holy shit. I have to take a deep breath. I feel like such a pussy. My eyes have filled with tears. There's no way I can cry. "I need to apologize to Mia for not being able to be the man she deserves at the beginning of this second chance we got. I've been given more second chances than anyone I know. I don't deserve them but I'm thankful for all of them. I won't take any of them for granted any longer. I've got a guardian angel watching over me now and I refuse to do anything to make her less than proud of me. I'm thankful to the men of Liquid Regret for staying by my side through everything. You're my family and I love you guys more than you'll ever know. We'll be heading back out on tour soon and I'd like to have Mia by my side. I'm in love with her and I can't imagine walking through this life without her."

The room is quiet for a second. I'm able to make eye contact with some of the media in the front row. The smiles I see put me at ease. I've opened myself up to criticism and judgment and I don't care. All that matters is that the lies are behind me and I'm able to look toward tomorrow with my head up. Harley always says fuck the haters. He lives his life the way he wants to. I'm taking a page from his book. It's time to start living.

"Max. Does this mean you're single?" A female reporter yells out and I can't help but laugh. Max just winks and nods his head. The man of few words thrust into the spotlight with my lie and coming out as America's most eligible bachelor. He's like a cat. He always lands on his feet. He's tall and blond and doesn't even recognize when women fall at his feet. His eyes are wide open now.

"How's Harley handling things?"

"What is Mia's last name?"

"Will you be getting married?"

"When will you go back out on tour?"

"Where is Oksana now?"

"Do the police have any leads on who killed Della?"

The questions are fired at us and we do our best to answer them. Harley's healing. We'd like to protect Mia's privacy and we'll take our relationship one day at a time. Oksana is heading out to shoot for a spread in a magazine. The investigation continues and we won't stop until someone pays for taking her from us. Tour dates are on hold at the moment. Max is grinning as I answer what I can. Every so often, his deep voice comes through the microphone with a short answer that gets their attention.

When we've had enough, we stand and wave before being led back to our cars. Security detail has increased for all of us. There are days I feel like I'm the president. I might even have more than he does at the moment. Until we find out what happened that night, we'll be more careful. Della's death will not go unsolved. There's no reality where that's an option. We've brought in our own experts to comb through evidence. The day they catch this sick bastard, we will all rejoice and know that Della can finally rest in peace.

Della used to always tell Harley that life was not meant to be wasted. Then when he took another drink, she'd pick him up and tell him that it was time to take a deep breath and start again. She was a stunning reminder of all the good in the world. A reflection of something perfect that was ripped from our lives for a reason we'll never fully understand. Every day I take a breath on this Earth will be a day closer to having some answers. All we can do is try to find our way out of this nightmare and start living again.

As Max folds his tall frame into the driver's seat of his Mercedes, a sense of peace settles over me. He smiles and I can see Della reflected back at me. Her smile, her enthusiasm, her zest for life. Max has had it all along. Maybe he's our gift from her. Maybe he's our reminder of the good in the world. I can't believe I haven't seen it before. No wonder they were drawn to each other. They have that same joy that radiates off of them.

The breeze picks up as Max drives away. I know its Della telling me I'm right. She's proud of me. I can't keep the smile from my lips. I know that whatever happens from here, we'll be alright.

Chapter 24

I sobbed for about an hour after the press conference. It was the most romantic thing he could've done. I know my life is about to change. Any freedom I might have had is over. But in its place is a relationship that I'd be willing to die for.

"Hey Mia." Harley stands in the doorway holding his guitar. He looks exhausted. "Last night here, huh?"

"Yeah. Back to work tomorrow. I'll miss being here with you guys though." I smile at him and he returns it.

"Want to sneak down to the beach with me? One last time?" His red eyes plead with me.

"Of course." I grab my sweatshirt and tiptoe behind him, out the back door and down the steps.

I'm giggling as we run out onto the beach. Lex would have a stroke if he knew we were down here. It's so dark and quiet. My giggle is contagious and Harley laughs.

"It feels good to laugh." He sits down on the stump and sighs. "I gave Lex the night off. The guys know we're down here. My face is my money maker. Better to not have my ass kicked for sneaking off."

"Your face is, huh? It must be a slow year. Let me know if you need to borrow any money." When his jaw drops, I belly laugh. I've been tiptoeing around him for so long that it's time for him to smile a little.

"Wow. I did not expect that." He laughs hard. It's a beautiful sound and I haven't heard it for so long.

"Get used to it, Griff. Haven't you heard? Laney and I are going out on tour with you for a week next month. Busting balls is her forte. Better wear your steel cup."

He just shakes his head, the smile bright on his face. "I've been working on a new song. Care if I play it?"

"I'd love that." When Harley starts playing the guitar, the wind picks up. I'm convinced that's Della. It happens every single time.

His fingers stop and he points at the water. "People suck. Who would throw out a beer bottle down here? Can you pick that up? You know I can't or.."

I walk over to where the water kisses the sand. I pick up the clear bottle and squint. "It's not a beer bottle. It looks like there's a message in it."

Harley laughs at me. I know I get excited over stuff that men don't get. But a message in a bottle? How romantic is that?

"What's in it?" Harley flips on the flashlight on his phone.

"I don't know." I giggle while I try to get the cork out of the top. "When I was a little girl, I saw the movie Message in a Bottle. It was heartbreaking but it's my favorite movie ever. I always wanted to find one of these. Maybe a letter to a long lost lover. Damien makes fun of me but I can't help it. I should have been a Disney princess. I want the whole fairytale."

The cork gives way with a pop and I dig for the paper inside. There's sand in the bottle and it spills out on me when I pull the scroll out. Harley holds the light over the paper as I unroll it. I just stare at it. I think I've forgotten how to breathe.

Harley strums his guitar while I stand frozen in place. The words 'will you marry me?' stare back at me. Damien's voice breaks through the darkness and my tears rush down my cheeks. My hands shake as I turn around and see Laney holding hands with my sister, both of them in tears. The men of Liquid Regret surround me and Damien takes a knee.

I listen to the words of the song and I know. I finally have my fairytale. I finally have my Prince Charming. I finally have the glass slipper.

Everything I've ever wanted is laid out in front of me.

One week was all, one week of time.
But in that week, you were all mine.
Free from pain, drugs and vice.
Free from grief and bad advice.
I know you're scared, my past is dark.
But the light you shine has left its mark.

Mia, not for a week, but til the end of time.
I want your heart, your soul, your mind.
To walk with me, to hold my hand.
to make with me, our fairytale land.

"Marry me, Mia?" Damien's hands shake as he holds the black velvet box. Inside, there is the most beautiful ring I have ever seen. The center diamond is square and full of fire. Tiny rubies are sprinkled around the band. It's breathtaking. But not as breathtaking as the man on his knees in front of me. He's my whole world.

I smile as I remember our first week together. I was captivated by his endless blue eyes. My fingers traced his tattoos, memorizing every colorful line. His dark hair was soft like silk and stuck up on top like he'd just gotten out of bed. I'd gotten lost in his bright smile. His laugh was music to my ears. And when he sang, my world was at peace. He was the sexiest man I had ever seen.

Now this incredible man was on his knee, asking me to be his wife. Asking me to share the rest of my life with him. Handing me the world. Giving me his heart. Letting me have the future I'd always dreamed up.

My hands cover my mouth as a sob escapes. I nod my head and jump up and down. "Yes. Yes, yes, yes!"

Damien pulls me to my knees and slides the ring on my finger. "I love you, Mia Avery Lee. I'm going to spend the rest of my life making sure you know that."

His lips meet mine as the rest of the world disappears. His kiss is soft and gentle. My hands hold his cheeks, anchoring him to me. Afraid if I open my eyes, this will all be a dream. He kisses my forehead, my cheeks, the tip of my nose.

"Look at me, princess. Let me see those beautiful green eyes." When I do, he smiles at me. "I don't want to spend one more day without you. You're the happily ever after I never thought I deserved."

I've never been so happy. I look down at the ring and back up at him. "You're really going to be my husband?" I bite my bottom lip.

He leans forward and sucks my lip into his mouth. I giggle and he groans. His voice is a whisper. "I'd like to start the honeymoon right now. But, I'm afraid I'd get my ass kicked. I'm not sure you've noticed your dad is right behind me."

I snap my head up and make eye contact with my parents. "Daddy!" I jump into his arms and he spins me around. "I can't believe you're here."

My mom rubs her hand over my hair. "We've been waiting forever for the call. When he left to go on tour, he told us he was going to marry you some day. We saw how you looked at each other. We had no doubt it would happen eventually."

I'm shocked. I look at Damien. "You told them that?"

He just shrugs. "I've always known it was you. I knew the first time you kissed me."

Harley laughs behind us. When I turn around, Laney slaps him on the shoulder. "What?" He rubs his shoulder and smiles at her.

I stand on my tip toes and kiss Damien again. Who says Prince Charming can't have spacers, tattoos, and a body made for sin?

Epilogue

We've been back out on tour for two weeks. Life is the new normal. Everything keeps going and then bam! Something reminds us of Della and we're thrown back into darkness. Mia took a leave of absence from work and has been on the road with us. Having her here has been good for all of us. She's the one we all lean on. She keeps us in line and helps us keep going.

Laney has been on and off the bus. She spends weekends with us if we're near LA. She spent a week on the East Coast with us. She makes Harley laugh and that means everything. I think Chance likes her more than he's willing to let on. It's going to be a wild ride, no matter what happens.

Oksana's popularity soared after the announcement. Her face is everywhere. She's spent some time on tour with us too. She and Harley seem to have a strange connection. Maybe he's still trying to save her. It was Della's quest and he seems to be honoring her memory by doing it. He's got good days but the bad seem to outnumber them. I know he's trying to start living again. But in those quiet times, when the bus is rolling to its next city and the rest of the world is asleep, I hear the nightmares and wish there was something I could do to make it better.

The grief counselor that was hired by the label has been a constant.

Rachel's cool. And talking to her definitely makes me feel better. Harley has pushed her away but she continues to try to reach him. Max's life has brightened since she's been around. I know they've spent a lot of counseling sessions dealing with his unresolved feelings for Dell. His healing is evident every day. I envy him for being able to move on and still be a whole person.

We just learned last night that there may be an eyewitness that saw something the night Della was killed. It's the first break we've had in weeks. We're all holding our breath. We want answers. We want justice. We want to be able to stop looking over our shoulders. Personally, I'll sleep better if I know Harley is safe. If I know there's not some psycho out there gunning for him, too. We'll check in with the detectives when we're in LA next weekend. They're close to solving this. I'd love to be home when they do.

"Why are you awake?" Mia stretches and turns the lamp on. "Another nightmare?"

"If I say yes, will you help me forget?" I smirk at her. I'll never get enough of her.

Her nails scratch across my chest and she bites my nipple. I'm instantly hard. It doesn't take much with her. My cock has a mind of its own. She's cooking breakfast? Yep, that's hot. She's painting her toes? Damien Jr really likes that. It doesn't matter where we are or what she's doing. I want her constantly. It's impossible to walk around in tight jeans when your cock insists on standing at attention anytime she's in the room.

Last week, she sucked me off in between sets. Knowing she was backstage cleaning up what her mouth had demanded from me was so fucking hot, I wasn't sure I'd make it through the whole show. When it was over, I slammed her up against the wall in the bathroom and fucked her hard. When I pulled out and saw both of our orgasms pouring down her legs, I was ready again. Joshua had to come looking for us so we didn't miss the bus. I couldn't stop. I needed her over and over again.

Two nights ago, we checked into a hotel on our night off. She stripped for me and demanded I jerk off watching her. When I was finished, she got herself off with a vibrator and I was hard again before she came.

Her body is a temple and I want to worship her every night. Every day.

She was made for me. We fit together like we're two pieces of one whole. I'm fucking exhausted. I rehearse every morning, make love to her every afternoon, perform for the world at night and then fuck her brains out until the sun comes up.

We're getting married in a few months and I can't wait to start our life as husband and wife. I want to have a huge family. Xander has spent a few nights with us and Mia's in love with him. The feeling is completely mutual. Claire has been pretty cool now that she's getting married to a man that treats them both really well. I've talked to Xander about having a brother or sister and he made me promise to give him a bunch of them. Challenge accepted.

"What are you thinking about?" Mia rubs my back and I pull her on top of me.

"Kids. Lots of them. I want to have a big family. I want to see you pregnant with our baby. Do you think ten is too many?"

She laughs, her eyes sparkling back at me. "I think we can negotiate a number we're both ok with."

"Want to start right now?" I wink at her.

She rubs her body against me. I can feel her nipples harden against my chest. I squeeze her perfect ass then run my fingers through her soaked pussy. She moans as she presses her body back into my hand.

"You want to come?" I whisper in her ear and she shivers. "That's it, baby. Take what you need."

She rides my fingers like her life depends on it. Her breathing comes in short spurts and I know she's close. I'll give her this one but the next one, she's going to ride my face. Her pleasure is too good to go to waste.

"Oh God." She arches her back off me and explodes on my fingers. As she's coming down from her high, I put my fingers in my mouth and lick them clean. My eyes roll back. Her flavor is a drug. I'm greedy and I need more.

"Climb on my face. I need more." I pull her sexy body to me and lick her from ass to clit. Her legs shake. "Ride me baby."

She rolls her hips as I lick and suck. She's so responsive and it doesn't take long before her thighs are squeezing my head and her scream echoes through the bus. I get so much shit from the guys but I can't help it. Let her wake them up. It's sexy as hell knowing I make her scream.

"I want you." She pants and grabs my cock.

"Take me." I hiss when she slides down my erection and squeezes me with her pussy. I feel her juices slide down my shaft. "Fuck that's good."

She pulls me up to sitting position and hugs me as her hips roll against me. Her lips nip at mine, her tongue explores my mouth. As her orgasm builds, she whimpers against me. I grab her hips and pick up our pace. I need her to come. I need to let go. I feel my orgasm building. It roars down my spine and as she yells my name, I explode into her.

We both collapse onto the bed. Our breathing is erratic and she closes her eyes. I kiss the inside of her wrist, her hand, her forehead. I don't ever want her to forget how much I love her.

I look around my tiny room at the back of the tour bus. Our shows are sold out. I have the woman of my dreams lying naked next to me. I'm living the life I've always wanted. I'm sober. I've forgiven my past. My tears are no longer Liquid Regret. They're filled with a promise of what tomorrow holds.

I'm living my fairytale, too. Mine is just a little dirtier.

The End

The Liquid Regret Series

Liquid Regret
Damien -2014

Liquid Courage
Harley - Early 2015

Liquid Assets
Max - Spring 2015

Liquid Redemption
Chance – Summer 2015

About the Author

MJ Carnal with Joshua Sean McCann,
Damien Reynolds from Llquid Regret.

USA TODAY Bestselling Author, MJ Carnal,
lives in South Carolina with her husband,
daughter, two dogs and four fish. If she
isn't writing, she can be found playing with
her daughter, watching The Walking Dead
with her husband, cheering on the South
Carolina Gamecocks, or obsessing over all
things Dr. Spencer Reid from Criminal
Minds. She loves to hear from readers and
writers. She can be reached at
mjcarnalauthor@aol.com, on Facebook at
www.facebook.com/mjcarnalauthor or on
twitter @mjcarnalauthor.

Acknowledgements and Thank Yous!!

FAMILY: To my hubby, THANK YOU for giving me all the "time away" I needed in order to finish this book. And, for taking care of our princess while I was glued to the computer. To C, you are my world. I love you to the moon and back a million trips. To my mom. Thank you for being my biggest supporter and cheerleader. I love you guys very much!

To Joshua Sean McCann. The day I saw your picture for the first time was the day I knew you HAD to be my Damien Reynolds. You were perfect and you were exactly what I pictured when I pictured Damien. You have added so much laughter to my life. I can't wait for all our travels together. To learn about Josh, visit www.facebook.com/joshuaseanmccannofficial

To Golden w/ FuriousFotog. I was dying to work with you and I'm so glad we got the chance. You are an amazing man with an amazing eye. I am in awe of your talent. I can't wait to work with you again and again in the future. You're amazing and I'm so glad we're friends. To learn more about Golden, visit www.facebook.com/furiousfotog

My cover designer, Marisa with Cover Me Darling, is AMAZING. I am so thankful we ran into each other in North Carolina. You had a great vision and you absolutely rocked the cover. (And all the covers from the Liquid Regret Series) Find out more about Cover Me, Darling, visit www.facebook.com/covermodarling

Kellie Montgomery! Thank you for editing my baby. Your kind words and encouragement always keep me going. Thank you for always believing in me.

Nathan Coy. You inspire me. Your words are beautiful. Your poetry is a gift. Always use it. Thank you for being my "official song writer" for Liquid Regret. Your friendship is a gift! You're amazing. (Even if you don't realize the SEC is the best)

To my PR reps, Angela Lane, Christine Stanley and the rest of The Hype

PR family. I love you guys. Thank you for believing in me and my books. I love being part of this amazing family! And Angela, I love how hard you work for me!!

There's no way I could list all the authors who have made a difference in my life in the past year. Being at signings and getting to meet the people I've fangirled over is awesome. Rachel Van Dyken, thank you for looking over the first chapter when I had it written and for giving me advice on how to make first person work for me. Thanks for reading this early and for being my favorite author in the world. Liz King, I love our lunches and dinners and any time we get to giggle together. It's wonderful to bounce ideas off of you. (and getting the inside scoop on your books is a major plus) Dawn Robertson, thanks for always talking me down from the ledge and for listening when I rant. Your friendship is awesome and your books kick ass. Harper Sloan, I want to be you when I grow up. Thanks for having an endless wealth of information any time I ask. And thanks for Maddox Locke. He's my book boyfriend, forever and ever. And to all the other authors I chat with, swap books with, rant to, and laugh with – THANK YOU for being in my life.

Chelle Bliss. Thank you for the awesome Mia and Damien graphics for the beginning of all the chapters. I love them so much. And I love City. But that's beside the point.

To my Moretti Men and Eric Wainwright. Thank you for continuing to support me on this journey. The Morettis will always be so special to me. I've loved traveling with Sam and Paul and can't wait to travel with Preston and Alex.

To my betas, Janelle and Ashley. You both rock my world. I would honestly be lost without you. I can't imagine anyone else reading for me!

To the Morettl Minions. I friggin love you guys. To the moon and back. Forever.

To all the blogs on my blog tour and all the ones who have supported me from the very beginning. Indie authors couldn't do what they do without your support. You have a thankless job sometimes but I hope you know I will always value you. You are the true rock stars on the literary world.

To my readers. I am in awe of every single one of you. Thank you is never enough. Never. If there were words stronger than that, I would use them. Having you along for this wild ride is amazing and I am thankful for each and every one of you. Your positive energy and kind words mean everything to me.

To the rest of my Liquid Regret Men: Lance Jones, Ripp Baker and Sam Jones. I'm so ready to take this journey with you!

I love you guys very much. THANK YOU!

CPSIA information can be obtained
at www.ICGtesting.com
Printed in the USA
LVHW011543210719
624774LV00014B/1042/P